DIRTY
DATES

DIRTY DATES
EROTIC FANTASIES FOR COUPLES

EDITED BY
RACHEL KRAMER BUSSEL

Published in the United States by Cleis Press, an imprint of Start Midnight, LLC, 101 Hudson Street, 37th Floor, Suite 3705, Jersey City, NJ 07302

Printed in the United States.
Cover design: Scott Idleman/Blink
Cover photograph: iStockphoto
Text design: Frank Wiedemann

First Edition.
10 9 8 7 6 5 4 3 2 1

Trade paper ISBN: 978-1-62778-145-9
E-book ISBN: 978-1-62778-150-3

Library of Congress Cataloging-in-Publication Data is available.

Contents

INTRODUCTION: KINKY IS AS KINKY DOES

What does it mean to be a "kinky couple?" Does it mean both partners hit the dungeon every night—or have one in their home? Does it mean wearing a collar? Does it mean a 24/7 BDSM lifestyle? Yes, yes, yes—and no.

The truth is, like so many aspects of sex, "kinky" is in the eye of the beholder. One half of a couple may be kinkier than the other—in fact, those kinds of stories often yield extremely powerful transformations.

If you were to pass some of these couples on the street, you might peg them immediately as a little bit naughty. Others, you'd stroll right by, without any sort of erotic antennae tuning in. Many of them take pains (pun intended) to hide their kinks— or exult in the thrill of maybe, possibly—hopefully—getting "found out."

The thrill here, what makes these dates "dirty" in the best sense, is the tension between tops and bottoms, doms (and plenty of dommes!) and subs, those craving control and those who desire nothing more than giving up control. Actually, there's a third category of sub, one who teeters on the edge between giving up and exhorting his or her own control. That fine line is teetered upon perfectly in "Switch," by Mina Murray, when narrator Cass notes: "He smiles, a sly look that does nothing to warm his eyes. That's when I start to get nervous." Keeping a sub on edge is all part of the kinky fun, but Murray makes it clear that this dom's mastery comes from the heart when he tells Cass of her new chains: "'I had them made especially for you. With padded cuffs, to protect that creamy-soft skin of yours. See how much I love you?'"

These couples act out their kink in many ways—some at play parties, some outdoors, some long distance. Some do it with bondage, spanking, service, a corset, a look, a location—for many, their instrument of choice is words. Emily Bingham takes one extremely charged word in "Magic Words" and lets readers know exactly what the prospect of saying it does to her character: "The shame is a scalding tickle that takes over every cell in my body. Looking down at his lap to hide from his gaze, I feel more embarrassed than in any naked-in-front-of-a-crowd nightmare. It's the one word I promised myself I would never say, yet he has managed to make even this taboo titillating, something I want to explore with him. I'm annoyed at myself for being so aroused by this lone, little word."

What is that magic word? You'll have to keep reading to find out. There's a sensual beauty to these stories that I believe will speak to those who practice kink in their lives and those who don't, because in some ways the tenderness, the charge, the power shifting back and forth between partners, transcends kink. It speaks to ideals of worship, wonder, adoration—from both sides. Even the most sadistic men and women whose worlds you're about to enter clearly value those they are asking to give them their bodies, their minds, their words, their beings. They are living out their most vivid fantasies with the person they most cherish. I hope you enjoy their dreams, fantasies and explorations, and that they inspire your own.

Rachel Kramer Bussel
Atlantic City, New Jersey

THE CORSET

Dorothy Freed

I want you to wear this to the party tonight," Duncan said. "You'll be the hottest woman there." Smiling, he handed me a gift-wrapped package and sat beside me on our sofa to watch me open it.

"Thank you, Sir, I can't *wait* to see what you've brought me," I said, smiling, addressing him in the deferential tone required of me by the rules of our relationship. I thought he looked pretty hot himself in a black jacket and T-shirt, with his thick dark hair combed back and his moustache freshly trimmed. I opened the package, drawing in my breath at the sight of the corset inside. I lifted it from the box. It was shiny black satin with lace trim at the top and bottom, with black garters attached.

"But Duncan, *look*," I protested, holding it up. "There are no cups for my breasts. They'll be naked." I felt a small shiver of fear. Silly as it sounded—considering I'd been Duncan's submissive for almost a year, and did what he told me to—I was still unwilling to bare my 36Ds at public functions, and so far had avoided doing so.

"You're right, Geri. What an oversight," he agreed, taking my hand and heading for our bedroom. "Let's put it on you and see how you look."

It took some major pulling and tugging on Duncan's part—with me holding my breath and sucking in my stomach while he laced up the corset tightly in back. He finished and turned me to the full-length mirror on my closet door, where I stood, barely breathing, staring at myself in awe.

Talk about an hourglass figure! Flexible metal bands sewn into the corset bent sharply inward, constricting my already trim waist, forcing my stomach in and my rib cage high. My generous asscheeks swelled outrageously from beneath the fringe of black lace that extended below my waist in back, and my pubic mound in front. My cunt lips, visible through sheer black panties, were plump and moist with excitement. Silky black stockings, secured by the garters, encased my legs.

But hot as the rest of me looked, my full, firm breasts took center stage that night. The metal-stiffened, lace-trimmed upper edge of the corset pressed them insistently upward, while an inch-wide satin tab between them kept them slightly apart. As a result, they jutted out before me—never mind my being in my late thirties—as high and proud as they were when they first developed years ago. They felt heavy and aching with excitement; my prominent nipples were hard, like little rocks.

Duncan teased them lightly with his fingers, smiling at my sharp intake of breath. Then he had me bend my head and lift my long curly hair out of the way while he buckled on my studded slave collar, securing it at the back of my neck with a heart-shaped lock. High heels and a black crushed-velvet coat completed my outfit.

He looked me over and nodded. "You look even hotter than I imagined. I can't wait to show you off. Let's go party."

"Like *this*?" I asked, hesitating, looking down at myself, then up at Duncan. There was just a hint of brat in my tone. After all, it was one thing to play kinky games with him alone, or with a compatible couple or two—scantily dressed or even naked when the play got going. I was up for that. But it was another thing entirely to walk into a party full of dominant men, leading with my breasts.

Duncan's look reminded me who was in charge. "*Exactly* like this, Geri," he said. His hand on my neck steered me to the door. "Let's go."

In spite of my concerns about my flagrantly sexy appearance, I was so aroused I could hardly speak—all the way from our San Francisco flat to our host's home in the Oakland Hills. Duncan instructed me to sit up straight in the car—as though I could sit any other way in this corset—and clipped a red plastic clothespin to each of my nipples. This sent a jolt of arousal through me that had me breathing hard and squirming on my seat the whole way over. I shot Duncan some pleading looks, which he chose to ignore. A truck passed us going over the bridge. I was too embarrassed to look up, but I think the driver saw me because the truck wheels, visible from the corner of my eye, stayed right beside us all the way across.

My nipples were stinging by the time we arrived. I attempted, with looks and whimpers, to guilt Duncan into taking the clothespins off, but he was unmoved. Taking my arm, he helped me from the car and assisted me up the well-lit walkway of a nearby house. I took small careful steps, because of the tightness of the corset, the four-inch heels—*and those damned clothes-pins*. My open coat barely covered my breasts, and instead brushed against them with each step I took, making me gasp. Blushing, I kept my eyes down and prayed no neighbors were watching. Duncan removed the clothespins before ringing the doorbell.

"Thank you, Sir," I said gratefully, wincing as the blood flow to my nipples resumed.

A bald man in black leather opened the door for us, checking me out with interest. Eyes downcast, I took a deep breath and hung on to Duncan, worried that he'd make me remove the coat immediately. He let me wear it into the dining room, allowing me to calm myself at the buffet table with brie, French bread and dark chocolate truffles.

The play space downstairs was huge, with a low-beamed ceiling; a sturdy redwood whipping post dominated the center of the room. Several couples were engaged in play when we entered. Most of the men were fully clothed. The women were in various stages of undress; all of them wore collars, and some were leashed.

Several feet to our left, a Rubenesque woman with jet-black hair was strapped naked to a spanking bench. *Thwack! Thwack!* The broad wooden paddle connected with the cheeks of her large, fleshy ass. She cried out plaintively with each stroke, asscheeks quivering.

To our right a movie-star-pretty blonde sat rope-bound to a kitchen chair, legs spread, arms behind her, with a ball gag in her mouth. Her top, a small muscular man with hawk-like features, was spanking her inner thighs and creamy pussy with a tiny red whip. The glazed look in her pale blue eyes told me she was flying. My clit pulsed and my breathing quickened as I watched the couple play.

Across the room two doms sat chatting on an overstuffed

sofa while enjoying blow jobs from the slaves kneeling at their feet. The insistent beat of the music was accompanied by squeals of pain and moans of pleasure—and the arousing sounds of hands and whips and paddles striking flesh.

"I'll take your coat now," Duncan said, reaching for it.

I don't know what came over me then; my disobedience wasn't planned, it just happened. Instead of handing Duncan my coat, *I resisted*—crossing my arms over my breasts and clutching my sleeves above my elbows, so the coat wouldn't slip off my shoulders.

"I'm cold, Sir," I said plaintively, looking up into his eyes. "Maybe I should keep it on awhile."

"Your *coat*, Geri." Duncan repeated. His tone brought me to my senses. I gave up the coat without further resistance—*and my big naked breasts burst into the room.*

I stood, eyelids lowered, hoping Duncan wasn't annoyed by my misbehavior, but of course he was. His eyebrows rose quizically. He cocked his head. The wry little smile at the corner of his mouth told me I'd broken an agreement and was in trouble. Reaching out, he took each of my nipples firmly between his thumbs and forefingers and pulled me to him.

"Bratty girl," he said softly, and took a pair of shiny, steel clamps from one of his pockets.

The clamps, connected by a foot-long chain, were the heavy-duty ones Duncan reserved for making strong statements. As always, his stern demeanor aroused me. I gazed up at him lovingly, regretting my defiance, longing to melt into him and be forgiven, but he wasn't letting me off that easily. I gasped and moaned from the intoxicating mix of pleasure and pain that rushed through me from the instant those clamps crushed down on my nipples. Grinning, Duncan clipped a short leash to the chain—and to my horror proceeded to lead me around the room.

"Hands behind your back," he said, turning to look at me. I obeyed instantly this time and my breasts jutted out even farther. They jiggled with each step I took, making the chain sway and tug at the clamps.

Duncan was enjoying the party, checking out the room, stopping to chat briefly with doms he knew—while I waited behind him like an inanimate object, my pussy wet, swollen and tingling with excitement. I flushed, certain that everyone looking at me knew how aroused I was. I kept my eyes downcast and followed Duncan closely, doing my best to avoid any further pull on those clamps.

When the grand tour was over, he led me to the whipping post. Smiling, he looped the leash handle over a hook above my head. Heart racing, I faced the post, which I was bound to by my nipples.

"Raise your arms over your head, Geri. Hold on to the leash."

"Yes, Sir," I said, and reached for it, grateful for something to hang on to. Mortified, I stood on display in the center of the room.

Duncan was behind me, his large hands cupping my breasts. I could feel his body heat and the hardness of his cock, which was pressing insistently against my ass through his clothing. My cunt clenched in response and my ass cheeks tightened. I moaned again, back arching, hips swaying, and rubbed my bottom up against his crotch, pleading to be fucked. His fingers teased my aching nipples, sending sharp little jolts of pleasure straight to my clit.

"Please, Sir," I murmured. "Please…"

"Not so fast, my darling," he said. "I'll let you know when I'm ready to fuck you."

Duncan stepped back and around the post. Facing me, he

reached out, smoothing the thick tangle of my hair with his fingers. Without warning he grabbed two fistfuls of it, pulling hard, forcing me to stand tall and taller still, until I was teetering on my toes, rib cage high and barely breathing. He bent, tilting my head back in order to bite at my pouty lower lip. He thrust his tongue into my mouth, licking at my teeth.

"Look at me." He released my hair and took a step back as I gazed into his dark, deep-set eyes.

"I brought you here tonight, Geri, to show off my beautiful, big-breasted woman. And that's what I intend to do," he whispered. "In fact, I want you to stand here and let everyone in this room admire you." He looked around, a little grin at one corner of his mouth. "I see several people admiring you right now. And that pleases me, my darling—because you are without doubt the hottest and most beautiful woman in this room—*and I own you.*"

He paused. "I'm going to whip you now for your show of attitude about the corset that *I* chose for you to wear—*and* for your deliberate refusal to remove your coat when I ordered you to. And everyone here tonight is welcome to watch. Do I hear any objections?"

My heart was pounding as I smiled into Duncan's eyes. There I was, chained to a post, humiliated, hurting, objectified in front of an entire roomful of people—*and more aroused*, I thought, *than ever before in my life.*

"No, Sir." I said, honestly. "No objections at all."

I can hardly describe how hot it was to be put on display in the midst of that party.

Duncan moved around behind me. Slipping his toy bag from his shoulder, he reached into it and selected a whip. He teased me with it first, caressing my back and ass and thighs with thin strands of black leather.

"Keep count and thank me after each stoke," he said, and without warning brought the whip down sharply against my flesh, where it landed with a slapping sound, making me yelp.

"One, Sir," I gasped. "Thank you, Sir."

I'd barely caught my breath when he delivered another stroke, then three in rapid succession—across my back, and generous asscheeks, and behind my sensitive upper thighs. These were followed by five more spaced wide apart—for which I was grateful—then five, fast and hard.

Duncan continued to whip me. My voice rose to a high-pitched squeal. Then, panting, I kept count of each stroke and thanked him for them—willing myself to remain still, to avoid extra punishment to my burning nipples. But when he paused to massage my reddened rear end, slipping knowing fingers beneath my soaking panties and up into the slickness between my legs, the exquisite sensations made my knees sag. The clips yanked at my nipples, causing me to yelp again.

By the time Duncan stopped whipping me, it seemed like I'd stood at that post forever—breasts aching, flesh flaming, pain and pleasure merging. Bathed in endorphins, every particle of me felt vibrant and alive with sensation.

I moaned, eyes closing as his fingers thrust into me. My back arched in response and the walls of my cunt contracted, clinging to him. It felt so good. I was gasping, flying, half fainting with delight. My excitement mounted, and when Duncan's other hand reached around and began rubbing my clit in that special rhythmic way he has, I exploded, screaming, into orgasm.

"Who do you belong to and who do you obey?" he demanded to know. He looked down at me lovingly.

"You, Sir," I whispered, looking into his eyes.

I screamed again when the clips came off. Duncan soothed my aching nipples with his warm, wet lips and tongue, turning the pain to pleasure. He loosened the corset, then held me for a long time, kissing and stroking me gently, caressing the tender places on my ass, calling me his good, good girl.

Later, we retired to a vacant couch where, bathed in afterglow, I knelt before Duncan, giving him head. I reflected on the events of the evening and the strange delight we shared. I'd never realized I was a big-time exhibitionist, but there was no denying it now.

Duncan knew that about me, I thought dreamily, my mouth filled with him, tasting him, breathing him in. *That's why he bought the braless corset, and made me remove the coat, and pushed me to my limits tonight.*

And that's why he's the Master. That's why I call him Sir.

THE SWAP

Jade A. Waters

Alex was a master when it came to tying Serena up. But tonight, it was her turn.

She could hardly handle her excitement as she waited for him to arrive home from work, which was only fifteen minutes away, allowing just enough time for her to finish setting up their bedroom with the appropriate rigging and gear. Alex had been perfecting their collection since he first bound her to the bed and screwed her two years ago—a three-hour marathon complete with his cuffs, her flogger, and an assortment of vibrators he'd used on her until she was wailing in ecstasy and succumbing to his every caress.

Serena loved being the compliant one, but every once in a while, she wondered what would happen if she took control. And last weekend, after Alex unhooked her neck from the bed strap and covered her flushed chest in the gentlest of kisses to follow the sweetest kinds of pain, he asked if there was anything more his princess wanted in a future session.

"I want to tie *you* up next time," she'd said.

Alex had thought about it for a minute before dragging his hand right back over her pussy, his fingers dipping into her in that way that said he was searching for her secret depths and wanting her to moan and writhe against him. Then he'd said, "Anything for you, my love."

And before he'd fucked her all over again, she'd told him the next weekend was hers to control.

Serena took a deep breath as she climbed onto her stepladder and remembered his touch. She'd never fully played the submissive role before she met Alex, but she'd also never been the dom, either. And here she was, a grin plastered on her face as she adjusted the eyelet screws she'd added on opposite walls of the room. Alex tended to hook her into the bed strap he'd purchased for her when they moved in together last year, and occasionally he bound her to a dining room chair. Other times he coiled her up on the floor of their living room, making it impossible for her to move as he snuck his fingers and tongue in the small spaces of exposed skin he left between the soft cords of rope, eventually bringing her to orgasm before he made love to her—bound, immobile and completely subject to his control.

But because she wanted this to be different—and also a little bit of a surprise—she'd spent a good thirty minutes in the hardware store yesterday picking out the sturdiest of eyelet screws. The clerk had shared a concerned look when she said, "I need it to withstand a lot of pressure from tugging, say, with a chain," but he'd found her exactly what she needed—that is, four screws, four six-foot lengths of chain, and some carabiners to fasten it all together.

Serena crawled back down the stepladder to gather the equipment, hooking four of the carabiners into the ends of the chain and then snapping them onto the screws near the ceiling and along the floor. She attached the last four carabiners to the loose ends, then took Alex's cuffs from their toy chest and laid them on the floor.

She glanced at the clock—Alex would be home any minute. She'd texted him an hour ago, warning him to be ready for a big surprise when he arrived.

So as he opened the front door and called to her, the delighted smile on her face when she came into the room didn't shock him at all.

"Glad you're home, honey," she said.

Alex set his bag on their drop table and gave her a quick look over. She was still in her own work clothes, and he pinched his eyebrows together in confusion. "I half expected you to be in some sort of getup when I got here," he said.

"Oh, I'm not done." She walked over to him. As usual, he wrapped his arms around her for a big kiss. And, also as usual, the way he twirled his tongue with hers sent tingles across her arms and made her instantly eager to strip down and comply with his every whim.

But not as usual, Serena squeezed his hip and pulled away.

"Assuming you're still okay with the plan," she said, winking, "I would suggest you take off your clothes."

Alex chuckled. "Here?"

"Yes, here," she said. She never giggled at Alex's requests—at least, not since they'd grown more serious about this whole kinky bondage game they loved to play—and she expected the same right back. "My turn. My rules." She bit her lip, enjoying the harsh tone she used to command him and the way he started the tiniest amount as she did it. "Now," she snapped.

Alex unbuttoned his shirt. When he tugged it from his chest and dropped his trousers to the floor, Serena nodded in approval. The bulge in his boxer-briefs told her he liked the game, so she stepped close enough for her chest to almost touch his and tilted her lips up toward his face.

"If you kiss me, I'll touch you," she said. It was one of his famous lines, and she delivered it with the same punch of temptation he did when he had her bound and whimpering beneath him.

Alex kissed her hard, and Serena cupped his dick through his underwear. He groaned against her mouth, then shifted his hips so he could rub more closely against her palm.

"Nope," she said, yanking her hand away. "That's not what I said. Now I guess I'll have to tie you down."

Alex's expression told her everything she wanted to know—how curious he was, how aroused he felt, and how surprised he was at the way she'd already flipped their roles around. She rubbed the thick wedge of his cock through the fabric again and he lurched in her hand.

"Jesus, I want you," he moaned.

"Soon. Here's what I want you to do, Alex." She leaned up to his ear, her heart racing as she ordered him around. This was so different, so much fun—never mind exciting, since her panties were already drenched at the images of what she had planned. "You're going to take off your underwear and close your eyes. I'm going to blindfold you and take you to the bedroom. Are you okay with this so far?"

Alex was good about asking her if she was all right with each stage of their bondage games, and she wanted him just as comfortable. So when he nodded and closed his eyes, she grabbed the blindfold she'd left on the coffee table and returned to find him rock hard. Serena gave a quiet gasp at the sight— Alex naked was always a treat, and here he was: submissive, eyes closed, and ready for her to play with—but she shook it off. She would have her way with him soon enough.

"Good boy," she said, reaching up to blindfold him. She

made sure to accidentally rub her hips against his crotch as she tied the fabric over his face, which sent the heat right between her legs. Serena reminded herself that as much as she wanted to bend over and have him fuck her right here in the living room, she had to carry out her plan. It was her one chance.

She took his wrists. "Follow me."

"Yes, Ma'am." Alex let her guide him around the corner and down the hall, and Serena enjoyed the rush of control. They got all the way to the bedroom where she made him stand in the middle of the carpet, then she wrapped the cuffs around his ankles and wrists, snugging the buckles against his skin.

"How are you?" she asked. She grinned at her boyfriend wearing nothing but cuffs. She'd been like this for him so many times, but this reversal was giving her chills.

"I'm good so far," he said, shaking his wrists about. He reached out for her but she dodged.

"Alex! Stand still," she said. When he pouted, she gave his thigh a smack.

"Tease," he muttered.

"Shh," she snapped. "Hold still."

Quickly, she grabbed each of the four carabiners and locked him into place. Within thirty seconds, she had her boyfriend splayed in the middle of their room, his arms and legs pointed at the walls and his rod straight out in front of him.

"Oh yum," she said.

"This is," Alex made the slightest of grins despite his covered eyes, "definitely different."

"Good. Different is good." Serena sidled up and wrapped her arms around his back, pulling him until his bulge rested against her. Damn, he felt good, but she had to concentrate. "I'm going to go shower now," she said.

"Wait, what?"

When she stepped back Alex slumped in the cuffs, but she keenly remembered the time he'd snapped her to the bed, rubbed her clit until she almost came, and then left her alone for an entire hour.

She wouldn't be that cruel.

"I'll be back," she said. Then she left the room and shut the door behind her.

"Unbelievable!" Alex shouted.

Serena chuckled, but she had some things to accomplish before they played more.

First, she wanted to clean up. She'd been so busy setting up after work that she hadn't had a chance to bathe, so she started the bathwater running. She dropped her favorite scent balls into the water and took down her hair, then stripped off her clothes and climbed in. She made sure to take her sweet time—exfoliating every inch of her legs, giving her pussy lips a good touch-up shave, and washing with the shampoo Alex said he loved to smell in her hair—and when she was close to being done, she called out to him.

"How are you doing, Alex?"

"Torture!" he yelled back. "If I could, baby, I'd tie you up and punish you for this."

Serena sank lower into the water and laughed. "Too bad!"

She was having way too much fun.

After a few more minutes, she glided her hands under the water and stroked her clit. She was already swollen, and even through the water, she could feel the slickness of her pussy. This whole idea had been spurring her all week, and though Alex was able to tie her up and leave her for a long time, she was getting bored.

She pulled the drain plug and climbed out. It was time for the fun part.

Serena threw a towel around herself and went into the guest room. She'd laid out the vinyl dress she'd bought a couple of months ago, the front and back panel connected by metal rings that made it impossible to wear any sort of underwear. She'd also left her lace-up boots in the room, plus a bottle of lube and her favorite vibrator. Alex had let her press the tip of it against his ass once when they were having sex, and he hadn't minded all that much.

Tonight she wanted to try more.

Serena put on the outfit, blushing at the increasing stickiness along her folds. Something about the vinyl on her skin, or the way she knew Alex nearly fainted whenever he saw her wearing it, made her halfway ready to jam the vibrator against her clit then and there. Instead she laced up the boots and scooped the lube and vibrator into her hand.

She knocked on the door to their bedroom with chills racing down her arms.

"Ready?" she asked.

"Finally," Alex said.

She opened the door. He'd obviously grown cold in her time away, but he still looked damn good naked and strung up in their bedroom. She stepped in front of him, the swishing of her hips making the vinyl rub and crinkle. He cocked his head.

"Are you wearing what I think you're wearing?"

Serena scooted close, letting her belly rub against his. He jumped at the cold feel of the vinyl, but then shoved himself against her.

"Yes, you are. I want to see. Please, Serena." He strained against his confinement, trying to get closer. "You are a real tease tonight."

Serena laughed, running her free hand over his hip and around to his ass. She squeezed it. "It's my turn, remember?"

"Yes."

"Are you still okay with this?"

Alex gulped. "I'm not sure what I'm saying yes to, but yes."

"Very good," she said. Then she smacked him on the ass as hard as she could. Alex grunted. "I'm going to take your blindfold off, but only because I want you to see everything I do to you as I take control. Do you understand?"

"Yes," he said.

She slid her hand up his belly, tracing her fingers in circles across the hairs that lined his skin. He was breathing rapidly, and his shaft had already started to fill with blood again, albeit slowly. Serena arched her hips forward so she could rub against him as she took off his blindfold. She left it around his neck, and when Alex stared down at her, he groaned.

"You look amazing in that dress," he said.

"Thank you," she said. "Now let's get to what I have planned."

She dropped to her knees, giving him a good view of her tits bulging out of the top of her dress. Alex moaned and pitched forward despite his restraints, trying to reach his crown to her lips, but she was an inch too far away—just as she'd intended.

"Like the view, lover?" she asked.

"Uh-huh." Alex licked his lips and she spread her legs until they formed a wider base beneath her. She was so wet at this point she worried she might drip onto the carpet. Her skirt had crept up on her thighs, and she glanced up to see Alex's eyes nearly rolling back in his head. "Fuck, baby..."

"Do you want to see me touch myself, Alex?" She already knew the answer but enjoyed watching his eager nod. She set the bottle of lube on the floor, then pushed the vibrator into her mouth and sucked on it. Alex fought against his cuffs.

"Oh, Serena—"

She circled the vibrator with her tongue. "I bet you want me to suck you like this, don't you?" she moaned. She pursed her lips around the toy, dipping it in and out of her mouth for emphasis.

Alex's cock was now at full mast again and she grinned.

"Mmm. God, I bet you'd feel *so* good between my lips." Talking like this was getting to him, but she was definitely dripping on the carpet.

Serena closed her lips over the vibrator again, then reached down. She shoved the hem of her skirt up, sitting way back on her heels so Alex could see her trail her fingers over her sex.

"I want to feel you." He was practically swallowing his own tongue. Serena took the vibrator farther into her mouth and flicked her fingers over herself—she was so riled she could probably come in about two minutes flat, but she wanted to save it for him. She snapped her hand away and pinched her nipples through the vinyl, loving the way Alex gasped.

She drew the vibrator from her mouth. "Only if you let me have my way."

"Yes, fine. Whatever you want." He shook his head and yanked on the cuffs. "Clearly, you have a plan."

"Oh yeah, I do," she said. She grabbed the bottle of lube and squirted some onto the vibrator. Alex's eyebrow raised.

Before he could say anything, she dove forward and took him into her mouth.

"Oh, *shit!*" he cried.

Serena's pussy quivered. She'd always loved swallowing Alex whole, feeling the way his shaft jerked against the roof of her mouth and how he bucked against her face. But this was uncanny. He was so hard, and he had no way to pin her down and truly thrust against her. Serena took him so far into her throat that her nose pressed into his abdomen, and when she peered up at him and inhaled against his flesh, she could swear he looked about to come. She pulled away.

"Can I add more?" She held the vibrator up and his eyes narrowed.

Slowly, though, he nodded.

"Your rules, right?" he whispered.

Serena curled a hand around his length, squeezing him as she moved her lips closer. "I'll be careful, sexy. And you'll like it."

She wrapped her lips around him again. Alex was already groaning as she circled his hips and slipped the vibrator between his cheeks. Maybe she wasn't supposed to be as excited as she was, but she couldn't help herself.

She took him all the way inside her mouth. Then she eased the lubed tip of the vibrator into his ass.

Alex grunted.

"You okay?" she said, her mouth full. It came out as "ou o-fay" but he understood.

He opened his eyes. His cheeks were flushed, his teeth gritted. "Yes. Slow."

Serena drew her mouth back, then slipped all the way down again. This alone was bound to make him come, but she used her thumb to flip on her vibrator.

Alex shuddered, his stomach trembling against her nose. She didn't move the vibrator from its placement inside his ass, instead working him with her mouth. He was throbbing against her tongue, and she was getting all riled up playing with him, controlling him. Alex tugged on the cuffs, the sound of the chains against the metal screws unbelievably tempting. Serena took him deep again, slamming the back of her throat against the head of his cock.

"Oh Serena, that feels so good."

She shifted the vibrator in a little farther as she slid along his length. Alex started to grind against her mouth, his breath growing more frenzied. She, too, was losing control of her breathing, wanting to devour him and feel him all at once. She moved the vibrator gently, in and out, marveling at the way her thrusts in made him jerk against the back of her throat. She was in control, and yet he still had so much of it himself as he pushed between her lips.

She wanted him so bad.

Serena held the vibrator still and dragged her lips away.

"No, no," he moaned. "Please baby."

She stood up and tucked her body close against his. His rod was like steel against her, and the heat between her thighs was making it awfully difficult to focus.

"Listen, sexy," she said, swaying against him. Alex took several frantic breaths as she pulsed the vibrator ever so slightly inside his ass. "I had this all mapped out, but I'm thinking you better fuck me, chained as you are. What do you think?"

"Yes!"

Serena dropped the vibrator on the floor. She turned her back to Alex and folded at the waist, keeping her hips close enough for him to slip into her and fuck her if he worked really hard.

Which he did. Dear god, did he ever.

Alex slid inside her and Serena yelped—he was so rigid she hardly had to move to feel the shudders sneaking straight into her belly. She leaned back as he arched forward, the chains snapping against the hooks on the wall.

"Come closer, please!"

"No!" she cried. She had to keep control, had to be in charge...had to put her hands on her clit, which was so swollen that when she swiped her fingertips over herself and he shoved himself as deep as he could go, her orgasm ripped right up out of nowhere and sent her moaning. She slammed back against

Alex and suddenly he was all moans and wails too, both of them bucking against each other as the pleasure ripped through them.

"Serena!"

She trembled, her vision blurry when he drove in one more time, the cracking of the chains sending a final ripple through her as she took him all the way in and howled.

"Oh, Alex!"

She pushed back, barely able to balance, using him as a perch. He had grown limp at the knees, and after they both gathered their breath, Serena turned to find his arms taut in the chains. His face was beet red, and his eyes shone with the sated look he usually got after taking control of her.

She kissed him.

"How'd you like that?" she whispered.

"It was different."

"Good different?" She ran her hands down his torso, admiring the way the chains pulled him so that the striations of his arms and chest showed. Serena draped herself against him.

"I think so," he said. He smiled and kissed her forehead. "But are you going to leave me like this forever, or what?"

Serena laughed, then unhooked his wrists. Tingles still ran through her, since she hadn't expected to come so hard from taking control of him.

As she unhooked his ankles, she asked, "When you tie me up, do you get off as much as I just did?" She stood up and met his gaze.

Alex rubbed his wrists, then threw his arms over her shoulders. He took a minute, skimming his hands along her forearms as he raked his stare over her dress. The fabric had crept over her hips and clung there, but she knew he didn't mind the clear view of her sex.

Suddenly, Alex grabbed her wrists and pinned them behind

her back. Serena gasped as he spun her around and reached for one of the discarded cuffs on the floor, its hook still attached to one of the chains on the wall.

He buckled it around her wrist and caught her ear in his lips.

"I don't know," he said. "But there's only one way to find out."

SLOW BURN

Morgan Sierra

Anyone who says he can receive a spanking without once flinching is a liar. Anticipation causes the flesh to tingle, every passing second stretching into an eternity. It's the wait that excites, that makes the heart pound. The knowledge of a need about to be fulfilled, an arousal of nerve endings, causes the body to tense. The very moment there is movement, any flimsy signal, expectation gives rise to flinching.

But to my Mistress, any such pulling away from her is an affront.

"I'm cross enough with you as it is," she says in a low voice. It is the one that lets me know I've pushed her too far. "I suggest you don't let your thoughts distract you from paying attention."

This woman dominates my every thought, draws from me every breath. When she walks into a room, I'm compelled to follow her, to linger on her every word. I want to protest that the world crumbling around my ankles wouldn't be enough to distract me from her. Instead, I keep the words to myself.

"What should we do about your continued defiance, pet?" she continues in that gentle tone.

I'm already so aroused it hurts, which is also a very good thing. For her, I would gladly suffer more. She knows what it does to me to listen to the purr in her voice. Even when she's voicing my inability to meet her expectations, the throaty sound tickles the inside of me.

She's standing behind me now, wearing the filmy skirt that splits down the middle along with a black turtleneck. The shirt clings to her frame, stretching over her breasts—breasts that I have worshipped—and over her flat belly and sides. Anytime she walks in that skirt, my gaze drops to the slit almost automatically. It teases the imagination of any man fortunate enough to lay eyes on it.

This evening, the contrast between covering her neck yet at the same time flashing the inside of her shapely thigh with a single move isn't lost to me. My Mistress is a lesson in contradiction.

Her eyes are blue like the waters of Barbados, her hair as dark as night. The thick crown of curls, along with an aristocratic bone structure, makes her seem like royalty. She's refined and dainty, a pixie compared to me. From the moment we met, her power overwhelmed me, and through a slow process of trust and giving, she has become my world.

The mirror gives me the opportunity to watch her if I'm careful, and it alone has often saved my sanity when I'm at odds over how to please her. When she's pushed me to the point of irretrievable lust, it is the mirror's reflection that has rescued me in the past. Don't ask me why, for I cannot explain it. Our time together is not always about sex, but about pleasing her. Through her satisfaction, I always receive my own.

I lift my head a fraction of an inch to gaze into the mirror—

not enough for her to notice, to be sure—because I can already feel the slip of my control.

"Eyes down!" she barks.

"Mistress." My gaze drops, but I haven't yet allowed my head to bow as it should. I want so much to please her, yet some part of me always rebels against this instinct. I was raised to be the dominator, not the one who submits. It's taken me almost fifteen years to realize submitting is the more natural of the two.

I used to wander, lost in myself, unable to understand why I never found fulfillment in my encounters with the opposite sex. I'd even tried sleeping with men for a while, thinking the answer might be there. The day I'd ventured into an online BDSM community, I knew I'd found my home.

"I truly have had enough of you, to the point I almost don't know what to do anymore."

"Mistress..."

"Don't. Not one word."

My mouth opens, ready to protest, partly because I do want her to listen to my argument, to know the disappointment I have in myself. "Present." There is a whip-like snap to her voice.

My body bows before my mind has caught up to her verbal command. Despite her obvious frustration with me right now, some things she has taught me well.

My testicles swing between my legs as I kneel on all fours. Slowly, I lower myself to my elbows, elevating my ass. She hasn't allowed my cock any relief, so it pokes me in the belly, a none-too-subtle reminder of my own frustration.

The sheets smell like sex, and more importantly, her. It takes strength of will to stifle a shudder every time I breathe it in. Others might not find it as intoxicating as I do, but knowing the satin has touched her bare pussy is enough to make me harder.

Every part of my Mistress is sweet, this place the sweetest of them all.

"I'm beginning to think you actually prefer to displease me, pet."

"No, Mistress." Nothing could be further from the truth. The reply escapes me before I remember she has ordered my silence.

"Then why do you hide yourself when I take from you what pleases me most?" Her fingernails scrape over the curve of my buttocks before she drags them down my thigh. "It's what you need."

She's right, of course. I'd sought her out, not the other way around.

Our very first time together, she'd taken me over her knees, rubbing my bottom until I relaxed under her hand. The slaps began as nothing more than little temptations of her palm meeting my clothed flesh. When after a few weeks of this treatment I was able to come at her order, I'd removed my clothing to avoid the mess. Then, when her hand wasn't enough to elicit such a strong reaction from me, we moved to a belt. After the belt, I'd graduated to a flogger. And then a cane.

I should be most respectful of the cane and the potential damage it can cause. Mistress is watching out for my safety when she instructs me not to pull away when she uses it. One misplaced hit could cause damage she has not intended. But I promise—being told to stay still and actually doing the same is an almost impossible task.

I tremble with the urge to hurtle myself off the bed and kiss her ankles or even the soles of her feet. My fingers curl into the satin sheets instead. Mistress is rubbing her hand over my buttocks now, and this is when the initial warnings fire in my brain.

I grit my teeth when a fingernail trails over sensitive nerve endings. I know what will come next. I expect the harsh sting of a slap. My entire body tightens, just as before, and I almost whimper. Already I know that she will not take my changing body language well.

"God damn it, Sean!" My name is an insult to my ears when the words leave her mouth. The bed shifts as she flees from it. "You will learn not to hide from me," she says, storming away.

The most awful silence fills the room, drowning me beneath its weight. I focus on my breathing to counter it, needing some balance to keep my fracturing sanity intact. It's a testament to how much control this woman has over me that when she walks away, even for a few seconds, the fear of her leaving forever grips me.

"Is this what it'll take?"

The bed dips as she climbs onto it again. I'm almost afraid to turn my face, but my Mistress has anticipated my hindered line of sight. She places the toy right next to my head. "It" is impossible to mistake, and my heart begins to race.

I hate the sight of it, but my cock thumps against my belly.

The black silicone plug glistens against the sheets. Perhaps she's already spread lube on it, readying it for use. This isn't one of the teasing ones, meant to press on that spot inside me that brings me to such fevered heights. More than once it's brought tears to my eyes as she inserted it all the way.

Her breasts press against my back, and she runs her fingers lightly over my skin in an affectionate manner. "Not so simple, pet. That will just be part of your punishment. There's more." Again, she has that purr in her voice. The one that makes me tingle.

She removes herself, and her scent, the freesia I've memorized, drifts away. Behind me there is noise that I do not recognize. But the delicious flowery aroma is soon back, along with the seductive weight of her clothed breasts on me.

Mistress pulls my cheeks apart and then presses something into me. My throat tightens and my vision swims. Fear grips me—fear that it is the black toy, despite the fact it's still sitting next to me.

I want to please her, to not cry out or clench against the discipline, but inside I'm trembling. The pain will be unbearable; I'm not ready. She's not prepared me. And I want the hurt, but I'm afraid of it. Even more afraid of displeasing her again.

"Haven't you earned this, pet?"

The thing is still pressing into me, but the expected burn from being stretched wider never comes. "I don't know what it is, Mistress."

There is a gratifying sensation awakening my nerve endings once the toy is fully seated.

"Do you know what ginger is used for, pet?"

The answer is so obvious, I'm afraid to voice it. "Cooking?"

Her laughter is beautiful. "Yes, cooking. But do you know what else it's used for?"

"No, Mistress."

"It's for bad pets who don't know when to release themselves to me. From now on, every time you flinch when you're being disciplined, I want you to remember today."

I still don't understand. Is it really ginger that is inside of me now? I know what the root looks like; the shape lends itself for insertion into various orifices. The pleasing, warm tingle whatever's inside me provides makes me wonder if I should flinch on purpose in future.

In truth, this new sensation has left me smiling. Mistress prefers a cooler climate in her bedroom and this new feeling of being so warm makes me relax into the bed.

"Does it feel good, pet?"

"Yes, Mistress."

"Then I want you to enjoy it. You may not come, and you may not remove it, but you're free to do anything else."

My entire body unclenches as I hear her words. I hadn't realized how tense I was being until then, but now that she sounds so happy with me, my cock thumps and I am similarly happy. Free to enjoy Mistress's toy, I rock my pelvis forward, allowing the toy to penetrate me just a little bit more.

"And pet?"

"Yes, Mistress?"

"You'll keep it in for twenty minutes. Not one minute less."

I don't have a watch on, nor can I see the clock, but Mistress takes care of me. She'll let me know when time is up.

In the back of my mind, something warns me that there is more to this than I realize, yet it eludes me.

I elevate myself on my knees, eyes closed, enjoying being filled this way. My cock is leaking, but Mistress doesn't punish me for this when it happens. She says it is physiology out of my control. Right now, I want to use this lubrication to slide my hand up and down my shaft, but I'm feeling so good, I'm cognizant that I might push myself too close to a ledge and not be able to return. No, best to just enjoy this.

I don't think more than a minute's passed before the warmth has heated even further. It's gone from enjoyable to just plain hot. Along my forehead, dots of perspiration begin to form.

Willing to walk the line of what she's permitted me to do, I glance into the mirror. There, I can see her reposed on one of her Queen Anne chairs, watching me. There is desire fanning in her eyes, and a slight smile on her face. "Mistress?"

"It will get worse." Her gaze flicks away from mine for a second, to the nightstand and then back. "Sixteen minutes to go."

I've stopped rocking my hips, realizing with dawning horror that all this time I'd let the ginger plug touch the insides of my cheeks by my motion. Already, those places are starting to become warm. Before long, they will begin to burn as much as the other parts it's touched do.

"It's called figging."

My gaze snaps to hers in the mirror. I spread my thighs apart, hoping to minimize the places the ginger touches. I have to swallow a few times to get my voice to work. "Mistress, it burns."

"But it will not damage you."

I believe her because she is my Mistress, and she has my trust. A single word separates me from true damage, from true pain that I cannot bear. If she is doing this, I am probably able to stand it.

Because I love my Mistress, I will.

This love is a horrible thing. I am constantly torn with the knowledge that if she knew the depth of my affection, our relationship would be over. It is my trust Mistress wants most of all—never, ever, my love.

At times when I'm caught in the euphoria—when Mistress has made me float from myself by giving me what I need, what only she can provide—I'm afraid I will blurt it out. That she will realize it and dismiss me from her sight forever.

"Fifteen minutes."

Only a minute has passed? How can that be? I am increasingly miserable, the sweat pouring down the sides of my face. Now I am pulsing around the ginger, grateful for the microseconds of relief that pushing out causes. When I writhe now, it is not to induce pleasure, but a desperate grasp to avoid the pain.

The bed dips beside me and I turn to face her. I won't beg with my lips, but in my eyes I know she can see me pleading.

Mistress strokes my face by way of reply. She looks back and then leans into me. "Fourteen minutes," she whispers, her breath teasing my skin.

I've spread my thighs as far apart as they will go, and I realize I am pushing the ginger out. My muscles tremble when I grit my teeth, and through a deep inhale, allow it to sink into me again.

I don't know whether to thrash to fight the burn, or if that would make it worse. To moan against the sensation or to cry? I fight to leave my body, but there is no place to go. I am hyper-sensitive to everything around me, my nipples and cock so erect they too are painful.

"Mistress, please, I can't..." I'm close to sobbing now. Mistress has seen my tears before and is unmoved by them. Her reaction does not stop them from forming.

"Shh, my pet. You can, I promise." She caresses my back, smoothing away the perspiration.

Mistress's hand slides to my chest, moving over my pectorals until she finds a turgid nipple. She pinches the tip between her thumb and forefinger, eliciting a small moan from me. When she moves to the other one, I'm already anticipating her, and wanting the distraction, needing it to focus my attention.

"Twelve minutes."

The countdown makes it worse—and better. If I don't know, I am tortured by that dearth. When she tells me, I am agonized by the idea of an eternity of this burning before me.

I am on fire and I won't survive it. My Mistress says I will, and for the first time, I wonder if she might be wrong. Our special word is on the tip of my tongue, ready to jump off and relieve me of this burden, but I struggle to hold it back, to not displease her.

My chest heaves as I draw in every breath, my abdomen flexing in response. My hips are still rocking, still thrusting my cock forward as I fuck the air. Despite the conflagration behind me, there is relief and heaven in front of me.

"Ten minutes. Very, *very* good, my pet." She kisses my shoulder, and it is as if I've won the lottery. "Now...how much do you want to make me happy?"

My teeth are clenched. Somehow I manage to push words through them. "With everything I am, Mistress."

"I like that."

She crawls forward, keeping her clothed body in contact with mine the entire time. Her mouth closes around my earlobe, and for a split second, I forget the burn as she suckles. My heart is thudding by the time she stops.

"You now have nine minutes, thirty-eight seconds to make yourself come. If you can't before the timer runs out, after a suitable recovery period, we'll do this again." The bed shifts again as she leaves my side. "Begin when you're ready."

My erection has flagged; the burning has driven all of my focus to the center of the fever. My hand is slick with sweat and trembling when I wrap it around my cock. "Mistress..." My voice cracks from the effort.

"Please me, pet."

And with those three little words, I recognize I have no choice. My initial strokes are short and jerky, designed strictly to help me refocus on what is my pleasure, instead of what is my pain.

It strikes me then that I have a literal pain in the ass. I start to grin at my own private joke, birthed from intense concentration.

The burst of amusement is enough to distract me, in a good way. I am getting harder, my body reacting to my Mistress's want. Eyes closed, I mentally follow the motion of my hand over my taut skin. It feels like velvet beneath my fingers.

"Eight minutes."

My hand tightens around my length, and my hips jerk away from the burning, toward the hand awakening my cock. I reach beneath it and squeeze my testicles, loving the tingling that envelops them. The burn has started to shift. It feels as though it runs up and down my thighs as well now, moving slowly toward my torso.

As my hand moves upward again, wrapping around the network of swollen veins, I open my eyes, searching for my Mistress. It is the power she has over me that makes the tingling strengthen. When I caress the base of the spongy head, my hips buck. When my ass clenches onto the ginger, I'm shocked to discover the same delicious tingling there too.

My mind is wrenched in two directions at once—screaming to get away from my tormentor, yet moaning to find my ecstasy. All too soon they are blurred, and I know not whether I'm trying to find the misery or the bliss. As the seconds and then minutes pass, I want them both.

"Five minutes."

I pull on my cock, running a blunt fingernail right beneath the slit, urging more pain to that sensitive place. My free hand travels to my nipple, still erect in the cool room, and then I twist. The bolt of surprise doesn't compare with what's burning me below, but it makes me harder. I am clenching around the ginger, trying to pull it in, and at the same time I am trying to shield my insides from it.

"Four minutes."

"My lady," I moan, for I am no closer to coming than I am to stopping the pain.

I am buzzed, feeling good mentally and physically. The pain drives the euphoria, taking me places I don't think I've ever ventured. Even when she flogs me with a cane, my most favorite way to be disciplined, it's nothing next to what I feel now. I want to worship the pain and I do as I keep stroking my cock, feeling so good, flying so high.

"Two minutes."

A teardrop of moisture beads at the top of my cock, and then spills over, drizzling down the side. My balls tighten along with everything along my spine. My asshole grips that ginger, pulling on it, kneading it. The burn feels so incredible, I want to cry out. I want more, *need* more so that I can come.

Deep in my center, all sensation pools. My attention sharpens to that one place. All of my roiling emotions tumble and whirl on each other, the pain pushing through the pleasure, which races along to more pain. Inside of me, a tingling, burning need pulls through my limbs and converges there, and soon I know I'm not enough to contain it. This fire needs to be set free and it will not wait.

"One—"

With a cry, my back bows as every muscle in my body tenses. The fire has found an escape, and it bursts forth, moving to the place where the pain and pleasure have met. I manage two more jerky strokes before the combined pleasure-pain explodes from my cock, ropes of come shooting forth and spraying onto the bed. It happens again and again until when at last it stops, I am so deprived of strength that I collapse against the comforter.

The bed dips next to me, and I drag my heavy lids open to meet my Mistress's gaze. I moan as she rolls me over and pries my cheeks apart. A riptide of pain shoots through me as the ginger is removed, but then the burn ebbs. My anus and cock are both still clenching, and I am surprised I have survived this test.

"You've done so well, pet."

I am too fatigued to answer, my tongue thick in my mouth. I want to tell her *thank you*, but it is all I can do to catch my breath.

"Now perhaps you won't try to hide yourself when I'm disciplining you."

Long minutes pass as she rubs my naked thigh. The scent of freesia is so lovely as I swim in delirium, I want to roll in it. I twist until I find her hand, and press my lips to it. "I love you," I murmur in a voice so soft, to my own ears the words make no sense.

Mistress touches my mouth. My cheek. She pushes my sweat-slickened hair away from my face. Her words are whispered and I'm so desperate for them, I grab on to the syllables, unwilling and unable to let them go. Putting her mouth next to my ear, she says, "I know."

My heart thumps wildly, my ultimate fear freed. That she doesn't push me away or leave me alone is all the security in what we are—who we are together—that I need.

As I lie there gathering my strength, I reflect on her words and on this night. I think about the price she's had me pay, and in truth, I'm not as sure as she is. If this slow burn is my punishment for deeds done or not done, then the next time we meet, I may have to find a way to displease her again. It could be worth it.

THE WORLD
IN MY PANTS

Valerie Alexander

It was almost midnight and the very loud band in the basement was taking a set break when Trey came into the bar. His rain-wet hair hung in his face and he had a guilty, furtive look, but none of that made him less heart-stoppingly beautiful as he looked around for me. He was wearing black jeans and a black jacket. And he was wearing his collar. The one I'd given him last year.

My heart began to bang in my chest like a caged dragon but I forced my eyes away from him and back to my friend Sophie, as if only focused on our conversation. As if I were too busy holding court in my dive-bar castle to notice Trey's entrance, even though almost every woman in the bar was eyeing him. He had that kind of presence.

"Is he here?" Sophie asked in a low voice.

"Right on cue."

I knew where he'd gone tonight. He'd gone to the one of the biggest fetish balls in L.A., in the hopes that I would be there, and had waited until it became clear I wouldn't be showing up. I'd already informed him I wasn't going but apparently Trey thought I would soften. He was wrong.

Last week Trey had sent a photo of his cock to my archrival, Lianna, or rather Mistress Lianna, as she made everyone in the local BDSM community call her. She'd always resented me, for the sole fact that my submissive boys were the prettiest in town, and she'd never been shy about trying to lure them over to her side—the B-list of femdom, as I called it. In the year I'd been with Trey, he had become her number one wish. And why wouldn't he? He was no average sub. From his full lips to his ripped body, he was conventionally gorgeous, but it was his collection of more subtle traits that made him irresistible, from that suspicious face he gave people he didn't know, to his beautifully boyish smile, to his silky, amber-colored hair. And of course, there was his cock. His thick, flawless, velvety cock.

Trey was new to BDSM—I was his first Mistress—but he was already famous around town for the prize between his legs. A few people had seen it on a modeling shoot he'd done; they'd gossiped about it and now he was something of a local legend. He'd tuck his head and smile bashfully when someone brought it up, and I was often congratulated on my "possession" of him. Such a beautiful boy, with the world in his pants. But I was just as often envied, and sometimes subtly reminded I wasn't quite as beautiful as he was; and of course there were dommes like Lianna, who itched to call him theirs, which normally I didn't think twice about. Until last week when, after being flattered by Lianna for months, he'd finally agreed to send her a photo of his cock. A complete naked portrait, actually, of him sprawled out on the sofa in nothing but his collar.

She began gloating about it all over town as soon as he

emailed it to her. It wasn't showing himself off that was the issue; I didn't care how many people he got naked for. It was the sneaking behind my back part that made me lose face—she knew that and he should have known it too. So I'd opted out of attending tonight's fetish ball with him leashed and collared like normal. There would be too much whispering, too many snickers, and I knew people would be more apt to forget about it if we weren't there. I'd told Trey yesterday that I wouldn't be going. "I can't go by myself," he'd pouted, and I'd replied, "I'm sure Lianna would love to collar you for the night. Me, I've got other plans."

Now here he stood in my favorite bar, a rough dive bar where he'd never been comfortable, with his collar around his neck and his green eyes full of desperation, searching me out to offer his heartfelt abjection, no doubt.

I leaned back against the bar in my fake leopard-skin coat and sipped my drink as if he were the last thing on my mind. This was my bar. I practically owned it, from a social hierarchy standpoint. Everyone knew who I was. No one fucked with me here, even though this was a bar of nightly brawls and smashed bottles and earsplitting bands and girls who looked like they could cut your heart out. Trey was intimidated here, which I'd always found secretly endearing.

Another friend, Cassie, approached me, but I couldn't help glancing away from her and at Trey, right as he saw me. The hope filling his eyes broke my heart and flooded my pussy at the same time.

"Well," I said as Trey came over. "Look what came in out of the rain."

"I'm sorry, Erica," he said.

He'd been saying that for days now. I didn't rehash my response, which had been screams along the lines of *Since when do you send naked photos to my enemies,* and *Maybe I should put that collar on the neck of a sub who'll be loyal to me,* and *Jesus, people tell you every day you're pretty, how much admiration and validation do you need?*

"How was the fetish ball?" I asked coolly.

Neither Cassie nor Sophie blinked. They weren't part of the BDSM community, but everyone in this bar had pretty much seen and heard it all.

"Pointless without you."

His eyes pleaded with me like a lost dog's. Then he pulled his leash out of his pocket and handed it to me.

My gaze met his. This meant I could do whatever I wanted to him. Not in the privacy of my living room when we got home, not in the accepting environment of a fetish ball after-party, but right here in this bar, surrounded by almost fifty people.

He was shaking—and not from the rain—as he gave a tiny nod.

I clicked the leash onto his collar's D-ring. A few people were watching curiously from the scratched-up wooden tables, but not as many as you'd think since a lot of crazy scenes went down in this bar. Trey started to kneel down to kiss my boots, and I clenched the leash in my fist, pulling him up short.

"No," I said. I unzipped his ridiculous jacket, because I knew he'd be shirtless under it and he was. Trey loved to wander through fetish balls bare-chested in just jeans and his collar, showing off his sculpted torso. Sophie and Cassie looked him over hungrily. Then I led him through the tables, past the band shuffling back in from their break, and into the ladies' room.

I don't think I really had a plan until I got in the restroom and saw the stall with the handwritten BROKEN sign on the door. A plan formed in my mind as a girl with bleached cropped hair straightened from the sink and looked with interest at him. "Cute. Yours?"

"For now."

I took my handcuffs out of my purse. I'd brought them tonight because I knew he'd track me down somewhere and, if forgiven, might wind up cuffed and naked in my car or in a deserted corner of the park. Instead I was improvising. I lifted his arms and cuffed them to the posts rising between the stall doors. Now he was bare-chested in leather jacket, collar and jeans. I had an idea of what I might find under those jeans. I pulled them down to his knees.

He was wearing powder-blue silk panties. Mine, of course.

The bleached blonde was watching with approval. Cassie and Sophie had joined us as well. A rockabilly girl I knew named Amy emerged from another stall and stopped short. "Whoa."

"He's being punished," I explained. "Beautiful boy, sweet boy, but not always that bright. And unfortunately there is no end to the amount of compliments and praise he requires. In fact, he sent a naked photo of himself to my worst enemy last week."

A chorus of condemnation rose up from the girls. "She kept asking!" Trey protested. "I'm not even into her like that, you know that, Erica!"

"Silence! No talking."

I turned to the mirror and smoothed crimson lipstick over my mouth, taking my time. I brushed out my straight black hair. Then I turned to him and put the lipstick on him too.

The girls laughed. His pale eyes flashed at them before he looked submissively at the tile floor.

"He is gorgeous," Amy said admiringly. "But he sounds like a greedy little slut."

She might have been referring to the photo he sent. Or

she might have been referring to the growing bulge inside his panties. His cock was swelling and pressing against the silk, pushing it out so far that his balls protruded on either side. We hadn't had sex since the naked photo debacle so I knew he was horny, and this was one of his very best dreams: exposed and degraded in front of a crowd of girls.

"Yes, that's exactly what he is," I agreed. "A narcissistic little slut. Why don't you label him, so the other girls know?"

I handed Amy the lipstick. She leaned in close to him and wrote SLUT on his stomach. Without even being asked, the peroxide blonde pulled out a purple eyeliner and wrote, FUCK PUPPY.

I glanced up at his face. His cheeks were scarlet with humiliation, but his pale eyes were turning dreamy and I knew he was sliding deep into that dazed ecstasy known as subspace.

Cassie slipped out and returned moments later with a team of more curious girls. The restroom was packed now. "That is hot," said a tiny redhead. "Who has something I can write with?" Amy handed her a lip liner and she wrote USE ME, I'M PRETTY.

"Jesus," Trey muttered, thrashing against the handcuffs. Maybe it was the tiny feathery strokes of her writing on his thighs, so close to his penis. But it was still speech.

"I told you not to talk," I commanded. I stuffed my lipstick between his teeth and told him to hold it without dropping it. Stepping back, I liked the picture he made: arms handcuffed over his head, leather jacket open and his hard cock straining at the scrap of silk between his legs.

A strapping rugby player seemed more competitive than lustful when she jeered, "So let's see that cock."

The truth was, we could already see it, flushed dark, iron-hard and sticking straight up from the panties. But I pulled the underwear down to his knees anyhow. He groaned with the delirious bliss of exhibitionism as the girls crowded around him.

"Give me your liquid eyeliner…"

They were writing all kinds of things on Trey now. In lipstick, ballpoint pen and eyeliner, the girls covered his thighs and chest and stomach, laughing every time his cock twitched. He arched his back, barely able to keep himself from thrusting his hardness at them, and then he did anyhow, wordlessly begging to be petted like a desperate kitten.

"So proud of that big cock," I said. I slapped it and Trey groaned; having his most sensitive body part slapped was one of his favorite punishments. I began palming him, rubbing, making him twist like a cat in heat. "Careful," I said. "Come on this floor and you'll clean it with your tongue."

"I want to touch his dick," Sophie said. "Do you mind?"

I could barely restrain a snicker as he immediately turned his hips her way, offering her his hardness, but she waited for my approval. "Go ahead," I said. "Anyone who wants to can play with his cock."

Which was how my poor sub wound up squirming against his cuffs, whimpering and groaning for mercy. His chest and stomach were damp with sweat, his face was as red as his cock, and his legs were shaking as he tried not to come. And just as I was about to take pity on him, a new girl pushed herself into the restroom and shouted about how she had to pee, and she would complain to the bouncers right now if we didn't clear the fuck out.

"Calm down," I told her and uncuffed Trey from the stall posts. I pulled his jeans up, knowing they'd be a little abrasive on that sensitive erection, and then cuffed his wrists behind him and pulled him by the leash out of the restroom. He stumbled after me. I knew he couldn't go back into the bar like that so I pushed him out that back door. The rain had stopped but the air was still heavy and wet. Two men smoking cigarettes looked at him in real astonishment but I continued pushing him forward in the alley as the door slammed shut behind us.

I guided him behind the first Dumpster I saw and leaned him against it, not caring if it hurt his bound wrists. My pussy was so wet and swollen I could barely walk.

"Please," he said. He sounded close to crying.

I pulled up my dress. He fell to his knees, licking my clit with desperate hunger. I balanced myself on his shoulders as his tongue washed over the swollen bud of my clit, rocking back and forth. My nipples ached in the misty night as I humped his mouth, so wet I felt like I couldn't inhale enough of him inside me. He drew my clit into his mouth and sucked it. Pussy worship was the center of his devotion and tonight of all nights I knew he was paying court to the galaxy of possibilities I had under my dress. He wasn't the only one with magic in his pants. But as much as I loved him, as expertly as he was licking me, I couldn't stop picturing his cock. How big it was. How hard and aching it had looked in the restroom.

I grabbed his hair and pulled him up to his feet. Holding the edge of the Dumpster, I climbed up on him and he pushed himself into my cunt with a broken cry of pure need. As it always did when we hadn't fucked in a few days, his dick felt colossal inside me, and I sighed with pleasure as I at last engulfed him completely.

I leaned my head against his. "Work for it."

He knew what to do. Leaning back against his cuffed hands, he used his hips to fuck me into a mindless animal euphoria. I pushed off of him just a bit, turning his thrusts fast and shallow for a few strokes, then sinking all the way down on him again. I wasn't going to last long and neither was he, especially in this position. But I drew it out as long as I could, torturing him, taking him to the edge and then making him wait again, all to remind him of everything irreplaceable I had and was. No Mistress was ever going to fuck or love or collar him like I could. I rocked him hard against the Dumpster, aroused by his wince as his cuffed wrists banged behind him. Then my face and body flooded with heat and I started to come in wet and messy throbs. I bit his shoulder hard and Trey groaned, unloading inside me with a shudder.

I let myself slide to the ground. I uncuffed him and we leaned against the Dumpster together, catching our breath until I felt a few raindrops splatter my face.

"Come on." I put the cuffs and leash away and tilted his pretty face up in the alley light. Between the rain and the sex and the makeup, Trey's face and chest were a rainbow-colored mess. A final touch of humiliation, really, as I led him back through the bar, where the last-call lights were on and everyone was looking bleary and rumpled. We got to my car out front just as the raindrops turned into one of those teeming downpours Los Angeles gets sometimes.

My windows were fogged as we got in. I looked at him.

"You're not done yet," I said. "You're making me pancakes tomorrow and serving them to me in bed. Then you're cleaning both bathrooms. Then you can go get me a gift and it had better be something I *love*. You can give it to me when we're eating a candlelit dinner on the patio tomorrow night."

He reached for my hand. "All of that and more," he said. "For as long as you'll have me."

The bar was closing. People were filing out into the rain, the drunker ones shouting with glee as they stomped through puddles. We stayed united behind our steamed windows as they disappeared into cabs and cars or hurried together down the street in huddles against the rain. At last the sidewalk outside the bar grew quiet and I started the engine, rolling the windows down to let that fresh rain air fill the car. Trey turned on the stereo and we held hands all the way home.

LYING DOWN

Kathleen Delaney-Adams

She presents her back to me, unadorned and shivering in the early morning air. I know she loathes being naked, the humility and vulnerability of it, so the fact that she's offered it to me has moved me greatly, made me rock hard. She is spectacular, standing in the middle of the living room, her eyes blinking sleepily, her body already melting in anticipation.

I have surprised her with this, barely allowing her to finish her first cup of coffee before ordering her to take off her clothes and give me her flesh. Although this is our ritual, a Sunday morning playdate we rarely, if ever, miss, I am usually gentle with her. I allow her to wake slowly and warm up to the day, serve her coffee in bed. The ways in which we arouse each other during these weekly assignations are myriad indeed, sometimes kinky, always juicy. This morning I want kink, demand it of her. Although this is unexpected, she has scurried to please me, collecting my whips, the lube, the condoms, arranging them within easy reach on the coffee table before she stands before me and offers herself up. She is eager for my instructions, always. I run my hand down the skin of her creamy back and murmur, "That's a good girl."

She quivers in response and raises her eyes to mine.

"I didn't say you could look at me, girl," I hiss, and we are on.

She knows the drill, eyes now downcast as she slips into her submission. There is a smirk of pleasure and excitement playing about her lips. I should punish her for her sass, but her morning face is so pretty that I decide to allow it. For now.

The first licks of my galley whip are a tease, a flirt of leather on her skin. Kisses promise more to come and render her shaking with desire and a bit of fear.

I like the fear. I let it build slowly, increasing the intensity of the lashes she is receiving until she moves her body in expectation of them, a slight shifting toward the whip. I laugh and hit her pussy, not gently. She moans and spreads her legs open for me, for more.

"Ooh, you liked that, didn't you, you whore?"

"Yes. Yes, Daddy." Her voice is breathy.

I hit her pussy again, harder, first with the tails then the handle of the whip. She is moaning louder now, gasping. She blinks back the first sign of real tears—tears of pain or need, I'm not sure—but I give her more nonetheless.

When I stop abruptly her body jerks in response, stiffening, then softening and leaning back toward me. She sniffles, and I flick the whip gently through her hair, letting it caress her long red curls as if it were my fingers touching her.

She has told me it makes her feel cherished, when I beat and whip her flesh, when I fuck her hard and without lube, when I make demands of her. But I want to remind her she is also cherished now, in between the pain—that my whip can be both a brutal weapon and a tender one.

I reach around with my hands and squeeze her tits, rubbing my thumbs over her nipples, tugging them. I slide slowly down her belly, my fingers finding her slick wet pussy. She cries out and stumbles, losing her balance, when I shove three fingers inside her.

"Mmm, nice and wet for me, just the way I like you."

Just as quickly I pull my hand away. My cock grows even stiffer when she cries out again and there is no mistaking her hunger.

I begin to whip her in earnest now, letting it build, slicing the whip into her skin with enough force to leave marks. That tender spot just under her ass is my favorite, the blood rising to the surface almost immediately in a sweet red welt.

She is fighting to stand still, moaning and sobbing, her entire body quaking. I land a series of intense blows on her back, and she sobs harder, in pain.

"Turn around," I growl, and she obeys immediately.

Her teary eyes meet mine, her mouth swollen and quivering, and I want to tear into it, bite it, draw blood. I can see juice on her thighs, her pussy glistening. Her eyes are pleading. I know she wants more. She doesn't have to beg—I'm not done yet—but I decide to make her anyway.

"Have you had enough, girl?" I ask. She starts to shake her head, than catches herself; she knows I prefer she answer me when I ask a question.

"N-no. No."

"Do you want more then? Tell me you want more."

"Yes. Yes, please. Please." Her begging is not part of our play. I know she means it, and I am so stiff for her I might explode.

"Lift your arms for me."

I demand full access to that delicate flesh. I want to devour her. Instead, I settle for my whip's access, the ferocity of my own need barely restrained as I slice the tender skin of her breasts, her stomach, her thighs. Her nipples are hard, her breath rasping, her lips trembling. She bites her lower lip to keep from crying but she can't stop the flow of tears, the sobs. When I lash out at her pussy, she again opens her legs for me, rocking her hips forward so I can better reach her clit, moving back and forth in time with the leather. This is a dance we have perfected over time, a dance not just of desire but of devotion.

I can't wait a moment longer to enter that tight pussy, and I lay down the whip and grab her, pressing her against me. She collapses in my arms, simply melting, and I feel her wet cheeks buried in my neck.

I hold her for a moment, allowing her to collect herself, my mouth against her hair, whispering soothing nonsense and inhaling her fragrance, the perfume of her hair intoxicating as always.

My hold on her becomes more insistent, more demanding, and she pulls back a fraction in acknowledgment before she wraps those mile-long legs around my waist and clings. I am torn for a moment between wanting to bend her over the chair where we stand and take her from behind, or carry her into our bedroom and spread her open in all her glory before me. The latter wins, and I carry her down the hall.

I toss her on her back on the bed, and she moves to make room for me, spreading her legs open without being asked. But I want her pretty little mouth first, and I tell her so as I yank my engorged cock out of my boxers. She scrambles to her knees, her fingers shaking as she unwraps the condom and pulls it over the tip, giggling a bit. She tears the condom with her nails nine times out of ten, but this morning it goes on smoothly, and she moves her hand up and down my shaft a few times, tugging rhythmically. I close my eyes to enjoy the ride. She licks my cock with her tongue, placing her lips on it gently, *too* gently, teasing and flirting. I love this game she plays, but today I am too far gone and I need her mouth on me *now*. I groan, grab her head with both hands, and force my cock in her mouth to its base. Immediately, she is gagging and choking on its girth, and so goddamn hot. It takes her a moment to regain herself before she pumps away at me, sucking for all she is worth.

"Touch yourself," I manage to say.

Her fingers slide over and into her pussy, and her juice begins to drip onto her legs and the sheets. God, I'm dying now with the need to release so badly. I come with a ferocity that makes my knees quake, and still her by holding her head again while my load shoots down her throat. Spit and snot and come and tears: her face looks gorgeous covered in my need.

I pull out, and without giving her time to wipe her face and mouth, I throw her onto her back and crouch above her. I pin her down by her throat with my hand, and begin to work my cock with the other, stroking and squeezing while she thrashes beneath me. I let her get desperate for it, for me, for my cock. I squeeze the head of it and shake it, splashing her tummy with her own spit. She is beautiful, splayed before me, and all mine. I don't need words to remind her of this; my possession of her was understood between us even before she became my wife. Mine.

The thought ignites me all the more, and I pull her thighs open farther and slide into her. She is so wet she doesn't need lube; I go in easily to my base and start pumping. She comes immediately, her scream of pleasure stifled in my shoulder, her pussy clenching hard around me. I don't want to come yet. I want to feel hers, to ride it out until her shudders begin to subside. I fuck her harder, faster, knowing it hurts her, knowing she likes it. She is shouting now, riding my thrusts, her nails and hands digging into my shoulders. When I finally come inside her she moans, "Yes, yes," and wraps all the more around me, pussy tight, legs around my waist, arms around my back. I fall hard on top of her, pinning her beneath me, both of us breathing raggedly.

After several minutes she nuzzles my neck with her face and whispers, "I love you."

I push up on my elbows and study her face.

"What a good, good girl you are." They're words she adores hearing. She's earned them.

"Did I make you feel good, darling?" she asks coyly, a flirtatious smile on her face. I wink at her, and stroke her cheek slowly with a finger.

"Oh, precious one, you aren't done yet."

Her eyes open wider, lighting up with understanding.

"Girl, you have one hole left. Roll over," I command.

She giggles delightedly as she complies.

THE RABBIT TRAP

Nik Havert

The bright-green egg stopped him in his tracks.

Ian had returned from the bakery with the hot cross buns Tina wanted. She thought they'd be a nice gift for the guy who lived alone two houses down and always took pride in clearing everyone's sidewalks with his snowblower each winter. She asked Ian to get the buns while she dug a card out of her basket of spare cards for every holiday and occasion.

He returned to find a lone, lime-green Easter egg in a simple white basket on the front steps of the house. He looked around the neighborhood. None of the local kids were out. There wasn't even any traffic. There was a note behind the egg.

Hope you can find the rest I left for you. E. Bunny.

It was Tina's handwriting.

He looked around again and saw another egg, this one dark blue, atop a shrub to the right of the front steps. He debated eating one of the two eggs he'd found, but it was unseasonably warm and he didn't know how long they'd sat outside. He put the blue egg in the basket and saw an egg drizzled with red coloring on the ground near the corner of the house. The next one was tucked under the hose guard on the west side of the house. The fourth was next to a paving stone on the walkway that led to the patio and garage. The fifth was atop a small pile of dead leaves to the right of the walkway. The sixth rested in the middle of the walkway, but something else was with it.

It was a pink ball gag sealed in a Ziploc bag. It was from Tina's beside table and he had no idea why it was in a Ziploc bag nor why she'd left it along the walkway next to another lime-green Easter egg. He put it and the egg in the basket and now looked around for her.

He spotted egg number seven instead. It was on the patio table and nestled atop a condom still in its wrapper. He knew by now that this Easter egg hunt was leading to him getting laid, so he actively searched for the next egg. It was under the tarp that covered their gas grill all winter. The canary-yellow egg was rubber banded to a small bottle of lube he also recognized from Tina's beside table.

The ninth egg was near another paving stone and accompanied by a double-A battery. Egg number ten, hidden on a windowsill, also had a battery with it. The eleventh egg leaned against the side door to the garage. It was in another Ziploc bag with Tina's blue vibrator. The garage door was ajar. He pushed it open.

He nearly dropped the basket—and his hot cross buns.

Tina had lashed a chain over one of the exposed roof beams in the garage. She'd clipped it together with a D-ring and slipped a pair of handcuffs through that. She stood topless under the chain with her arms over her head, wrists secured in the cuffs, and wearing a pair of white lace panties adorned with a cotton-tail. Her headband was topped with fluffy costume rabbit ears. Her feet were in bunny slippers he'd never seen before and spread wide to two concrete blocks. She'd wrapped each block in another chain, D-ring, and handcuffs combination. The twelfth egg and a handcuff key were between her feet.

She looked back at him with pleading eyes.

"Please, mister, you've got to let me out of this trap. I'm the Easter Bunny!"

Ian blinked a couple times, got over the initial shock and set down the box of buns on a nearby shelf.

"You are?"

"Yes, and you've got to let me loose. I have a lot more eggs to deliver. You know, it's really mean of you to set a trap like this for rabbits like me."

"Well, I've caught you nonetheless," Ian said as he put the Easter basket between her feet. "Do I get three wishes?"

"Those are leprechauns. I'm the Easter Bunny. You have to let me go."

"Really?" He pressed against her back. He saw her arms twitch. "Maybe I should keep you here. Rabbit is rather tasty."

She looked back at him with feigned fear. "You're going to eat me?"

He yanked her panties down to her knees. He knelt behind her and pulled her back by the hips. His tongue slipped into her and she let out one of her long groans that always turned him on. She was so wet from the anticipation of her little game that he wasn't sure he'd need the lube. He tickled her clit while he licked her top to bottom. He playfully bit her ass and then gave it a quick spank. She screamed and then tried to look back at him.

"You're so mean. How can you do this to me? Don't you know who I am?"

He stood up and put the ball gag in her mouth. "Yes. You're the rather talkative Easter Bunny who's been caught in my garage. As far as I can tell, you're mine now and I can do what I like with you."

She shook her head. He could see sweat beading on her throat and he reached around to give her nipples a hard pinch. She jerked her ass back against him and rubbed his cock through his jeans. He tugged her hair, making her grunt in satisfaction.

"This is about what I want, not what you want. If you want me to let you go, then you'll have to convince me that I shouldn't just keep you here."

He got undressed while she attempted to turn her head to see where he was. He rolled the condom onto his cock and then doused it with the lube. He put the batteries in her vibrator and twisted the dial. The sound snapped her to attention as he gently dragged it over her waiting cunt. She tried to grind on it, but he moved it away before she could get it deeper inside her pussy. When he drizzled lube over her ass, she started another long moan through the ball gag.

He pressed against her from behind so his cock could slide up and down between her oiled cheeks. He drew a line down her spine with the vibrator. "I guess since I don't get three wishes I'll take something else."

He slipped into her ass without much trouble. The angle was a bit awkward at first, but she'd made the chain above her head long enough that she could bend over a bit. He almost pulled out right away. She was hotter than she'd been in weeks. He took a deep breath and pushed farther until his belly rubbed against her slick bottom. He put the vibrator on her clit. It was one of her favorite things—him balls deep in her ass with her clit buzzing and unable to stop it.

She went rigid as she came. He rocked back until just the head of his cock was in her. She bit down on the ball gag and yelled a high-pitched wail as she soaked his balls with come. She snapped out of her trance and he plunged back up her ass as her hips went wild. He slapped against her and did just what he said he would—he took her ass. He took it until he felt like someone was tickling his balls with a sparkler. He pulled out, tore off the condom, and gave her the finish she always wanted. He coated her ass with his come. He sprayed her with four thick streams but knew he wasn't done.

He slipped his sore cock into her wet cunt and worked the vibrator up her ass while they both still had energy. He fucked her ass with the vibrator and let her work over his cock as much as she wanted. She kept screaming and he was thankful she'd remembered the ball gag because otherwise he was certain the neighbors would've called the cops by now.

He caught a glimpse of her eyes and saw they had rolled upward; her eyelids were fluttering faster than a butterfly's wings. He pulled out the vibrator and dropped it into the basket between her feet. He removed the gag, leaving her mouth a gasping, drooling mess. Her hips slowly calmed and his aching cock slipped from her.

He uncuffed her and then grabbed a stool from near his workbench. She almost collapsed onto it and had to lean against his chest to keep from falling to the floor.

"Happy Easter," she said.

"You too," he said. "And I hadn't even given you your present yet."

"That wasn't it?"

"I figured that was mine. Yours is in the house."

She perked up. "What is it?"

He grinned. "You might not want it now."

"I'll probably want it more. What is it?"

He grinned wider. "A vibrating egg."

She grinned even wider.

CLOSING TIME

Elise Hepner

Another order of pancakes and then closing time, Mrs. Evans. I don't want to hear any lip about it." Max poured a cup of coffee and tossed a mixed omelet on the grill. "It's a holiday; we're closing early for a celebration. If I don't make it worth your while you have full permission to turn off the big game tomorrow and ban me from watching it while I paint your toes and draw you a bubble bath."

My husband drove home his dare by crossing behind the diner counter and covertly cupping my jeans-clad ass in his large palm. The heat of him through my clothes pressed against me, as if he was going to force me to bend over the counter and take me doggy-style in front of the customers. I wished the images in my head were a promise, more than a fantasy. But before anyone could see him get too fresh, I swatted his hand away with the dish towel slung in my pocket. Max chuckled, sauntering away with a whistle. The damn man didn't know the first thing about waiting tables or doing the books—but fuck if his charm didn't sell food as if we were back in the Great Depression.

Despite the fact that our place was teeming with customers—thanks to Autumn Weekend Resplendence, our small town's annual pre-Thanksgiving festival—I couldn't be more anxious for their crumpled bills to pass through my fingers so I could have one second alone with Max. While running a steady business fulfilled me, being rammed up against the counter when the lights were out would take our anniversary to a whole new level. We'd skipped our holiday the past two years in favor of getting more hours and thus more customers to pay back our loans for the diner. There was a lot of time to make up for—which is why my husband's proposal was so enticing.

And tonight was fixing to be an extraordinary occasion.

At least if Max's brag had any truth to it.

"Get to mixing burgers in the back, slave. It's the only thing you're good for, ya know!" I called down the line of the counter and my husband popped his head out of the doorway. His challenging look sent a chill through all my nerve endings, which were on high alert. A flush colored my cheeks and I could sense it crawling up my face until I was as red as a bicycle brake light.

Max gave one shake of his head—a warning. His eyes narrowed with personal, dangerous intent—and I hoped to experience everything that loaded action conveyed tonight. Damn, I needed to get my head in the right place and out of his boxers. In my mind his cock was already shoved to the hilt in my mouth, making me cry for mercy while he fucked my face.

A good Southern girl can be just as bad as the devil—I know firsthand.

The loud buzz of conversation reminded me to work faster as I struggled with the machine of death, a fond moniker for the cappuccino maker my determined husband insisted we import from some country in Europe. "The haughty coffee crowd will come in droves," he'd insisted. "We'll rival the only other coffee place in town." All lovely arguments—except for the fact that he hadn't touched the manual with a ten-foot pole since we had it delivered and set up, which made me coffee's bitch for the night. Plus every other day someone ordered a froufrou drink with more dairy than caffeine, something I dreaded. My hands shook as steam pulsed out of the machine, caressing my face in puffs of unbearable heat.

Maybe all the work had gone to my head, but for a beat, the blistering heat cradling my cheek made me miss Max's hand cupped against my face. It'd been so long since we'd had more than a caress to ourselves. No one had told me that as a business owner, sleep would be my prime objective. More sacred than sex—no matter what the orifice—and that was saying something. With a mutter, I shook my head and poured milk into the latte with all the expertise of a shaking five-year-old holding a gallon jug. I didn't even dare to blink, lest I mess it up—again.

The whipped cream toppled out of the can in a lump into the recyclable cup. At least it would be covered. I donned the paper cup's top and slid it over to the customer who had her money waiting on the edge of the counter and a small frown tipping her eyebrows into bat wings.

"You have a good writing session today, Mrs. Dobison. Let me know if you need me to do any late-night deliveries since you're on deadline."

All I got back was a jumble of words that could have been a brainstorm, before she tucked her down coat around her middle and shuffled out. I loved her anyway—she single-handedly kept our coffee shop in business with a nine-cup-a-day habit. The day she dropped dead from stress we were selling the machine of death to buy new antique booths for the corner tables. I'd rather have old than new any day of the week.

After the nightly rush and the stragglers had been wrangled out by Max with the promise of blueberry pie in the morning, there was only him, the cash that needed to be sorted and me. The mystery of whatever he had planned for tonight streamed through my thoughts in Technicolor. My fingertips itched to rip open his plaid shirt roughly enough that the buttons went scattering so far customers would be finding them for weeks.

But that wasn't how we worked.

Instead my hands remained shaking, palms down on the cool counter while the rest of me burned with arousal, a pulsing need that made my inner pussy muscles flutter and shoved my heart square inside my throat. My gaze locked on Max's firm ass as he locked our doors for the night. Our apartment was upstairs, but as adrenaline coursed through my center, making my head slightly fuzzy, my husband made his way across the linoleum.

He had *the* look—the one that always makes my toes curl in my ballet flats. His dark hair was mussed, while his cerulean-blue eyes honed in on me as if he could see my every desire and rip my clothes off with the intensity of his stare. A slow half-smirk showed his left dimple, and that slow seductive stalk that moved his hips as if he was a predator almost brought me to my knees. The hairs on the nape of my neck prickled, sending a flip low in my belly. Without noticing I was doing it, I was using the diner counter as a crutch, more than any particular show of submission.

My heart nearly stopped when Max jumped up onto the counter an inch away from my hands, slid across it until he was behind me, then pressed his hand between my legs. As he cupped my pussy, a gasp tore out of my tight chest. He massaged me hard enough to almost bruise my labia and mound through my pants—not that I minded one bit. His rough, relentless fondling pressed my stomach against the vinyl checkered countertop until the edge bit into me enough that my hands scrambled for purchase on the slick surface. My husband manhandled me like he was frisking my pussy for possible possession of a bowie knife as excitement chased up my body, making my thoughts turn the consistency of cheap vanilla pudding.

I didn't think about protesting. His hand was already buried deep into my brown ringlets so his nails scraped my scalp, anchoring me while also easing me away from the counter and forcing me to turn around with a wince. My every breath was a choppy sip of air that smelled like pie and rolled around in my mouth like pure sex. He licked his lips, finger gliding along my slick clit as I hissed and shuddered despite his tight hold.

Our eyes locked, his brows raised as if waiting for me to tap out. Fat chance. I did the one thing I could to push his buttons good and hard: I stuck my small, pink tongue out at him—then all but salivated for his well-timed revenge. He couldn't ignore me. Max could—and would—take pleasure in teaching me a lesson as the diner lights blazed behind us. He didn't waste a second in ripping his hand out of the front of my pants, so quickly I didn't have time to make a sound or regret the loss of him.

He bent me backward against the diner counter until my whole upper body slammed down and the roughness knocked the breath out of me. But I didn't scramble away. My nipples hardened against my shirt and my panties grew so damp I pressed my thighs together. Even as Max nudged in between them, his hard cock pressed against my core. With my head pinned at an awkward angle and his nails still digging into my scalp, I opened my legs in silent invitation for whatever he wanted to dish up. All the fight in me was reined in because he fought back with every press against my naughty bits.

"Don't. Move. A. Muscle."

His low, seething menace had the same effect as if he'd rubbed his hands all along the forbidden spots of my body with his tongue and teeth. Goose bumps tickled across my flesh and I licked my lips. A growl low in his throat twisted in my abdomen. I begged him without any words to separate the half inch between our mouths so I could taste him. When he pivoted away from me, I slung my hands over my head to grip the other side of the counter. Old habits die hard. I'd want to have a good hold for this ride.

From my angle I couldn't see what he was doing over by the double grill combination, but the harsh yellow lighting from above made me blink. Reality set in hard and fast in the span of that small movement. We hadn't turned out the lights for the night. Our diner was parked in the center of town, right across from the town square, with our lights blazing bright while Max all but harassed me on our diner countertop in front of the large picture windows—and I was ready to beg for more.

Christ on a cracker. I sent up a silent prayer that Riley, the town sheriff, wasn't patrolling before Max turned back to me with a little laugh. My lips tightened to a thin line; the busybody in me wanted to ask him what was so funny, but deep down I knew nothing was really funny—he laughed low and throaty when he got extra horny. Sometimes he even did it while he was coming, as if he couldn't keep the joy in his body any longer. His sex laugh was one of the sexiest sounds I'd ever been lucky enough to hear.

Tonight he wasn't screwing around—he made that extra clear when a sharp butcher's blade shone unmistakably in the harsh diner light. My pulse roared against my temples. He didn't hesitate and I didn't dare breathe while the sharp kitchen utensil ripped through the bottom of my cotton T-shirt. He angled the blade upward, cutting with a not so surprising accuracy and gentle efficiency until my shirt was split nearly to my neck. Without a single look at my pale, surprised expression, he half-turned back and shoved the knife in the holder hard enough for it to vibrate against the counter.

Max's large hands tore what little was left of the shirt off my body without pause. I cried out, unsure what to do. But he didn't leave me any choice as he manhandled the scraps off my arms until he could throw the tattered fabric to the ground. I'd been married to my husband for over ten years but I'd never experienced the bone-deep edginess he gave off tonight, as if he couldn't consume me quick enough. When I gathered the courage to trace my gaze past his upper body, which was practically vibrating with primal sensuality, I lingered on a patch of stubble he'd missed that morning when he'd shaved half-asleep.

Though I knew his body, along with its patterns and quirks, as well as I knew my own, there was nothing readable in his eyes. Nothing to show me the way our night was going to turn out. I might as well have been fucking a stranger. And that's when he backhanded me. Not hard enough to see stars, but the sting sculpted to my jaw until my flesh was on fire and I was sure there was a handprint left on my skin.

Blink. Blink. I worked my jaw up and down. Shock turned to a surprising amount of arousal in the snap of a finger as blazing rage made my nipples tighten in my flimsy excuse for a bra. Muscles I didn't know I had tightened with indignant, rash intensity. I glared up at him with the faint spatter of goose bumps all over my flesh. He cocked his head to the side before pressing his full lips into a single air kiss.

"Internet history is a funny little toy, don't you think?"

"How—"

Both of his hands pulled down my bra cups, tucking them beneath my breasts, allowing him to slap my right nipple hard enough that I bucked off the table despite my hold on it. An instant wetness suffused my pussy while my mind was only beginning to process his actions. A low rumble echoed in his chest. I lay stinging and vulnerable as he repeated his rash action against my other breast. My flesh jiggled, even though this blow was no less surprising.

"I know you like it. I saw all the sites. I pay attention. I've got to be a dutiful husband worthy of my wife." While his actual words were sweet, he whispered them against the lip of my ear as if they were nasty, vile suggestions. "I'm always one step ahead, baby. Don't try to keep secrets."

Even knowing his next move didn't prepare me for the harsh shudder that bowed my spine as pain white-knuckled my fingers against the counter at my head. Another set of slaps and my stomach twisted into knots. Heat rose beneath my flesh. I squeezed my eyes tightly shut, focusing on the central knot of agony hammering through my nerve endings. My pussy muscles fluttered as my nipples stung and pulsed with the slow burn of his palm print.

His next slap landed against my hip bone and snapped my eyes open, watching his lips twist with the sheen of sweat along the sharp plains of his face. My throat was tight, a wash of fever whipping beneath my flesh. I couldn't quite move past the hop-skip of my thoughts, unable to understand how we'd progressed from light BDSM and role-playing to the harsh, pleasurable sting of his palm on my flesh while the lights of our diner high-lighted the bright-pink sting against my skin.

"Everyone can see you. I'm sure you love being the little attention whore that you truly are. Stay still and you'll get what you want—if I'm feeling generous."

He stroked over my breasts and slid down beneath the waist of my jeans, roughly cupping my pussy. I squirmed against the unpredictable pressure and friction of his fingers trapped against my plain cotton panties. He squeezed me so hard I bucked up and thought I might come right then and there. Max pushed aside my panties, working one of his thick fingers inside my cunt as I writhed and wiggled for more of him inside me.

As he claimed me, excitement ignited the lust behind his stare. His unshakeable desire made every inch of him shiny and new even after all our years together. Max used one hand to unsnap my jeans and shove them down to my ankles, turning them into makeshift bonds keeping my legs in place. He was close—only an inch away from me—but wherever his blows landed they weren't enough to keep the acute need at bay. He would never be close enough. These little teases only cracked open the door to something so much better, a new world of tantalizing pleasure that would be doled out at my husband's whim.

"I think you can take more." He grabbed my inner thigh until I winced and tried to wiggle—whether away or farther into him, I couldn't be sure yet. My mind was only impulse and action without rationality. I needed—craved. Cool air eased along my naked flesh as if it were a heavy weight taunting every muscle, while I pulsed and twitched from Max's well doled out, careful abuse.

I arched to meet his palm as he slapped against my mound and half of my clit while I relished the ecstasy that washed up with each strike.

Another. And another—random, non-rhythmic blows that only brought my lust up to the surface of my skin and did nothing to ease my ache or release the tension wound like a knot in my tummy.

"Please tell me you're going to fuck me. I need you to fuck me. Come on, please?"

"In due time." His laughter was like homemade taffy sticking to my insides.

My legs trembled, heels tapping against the side of the counter while the air-conditioning washed against my arousal. I couldn't decide whether I'd rather have another slap or nothing at all. My gaze strayed past the lit windows. My head tilted back so blood rushed to my temples and dizziness washed over me.

In the sheen through the oversized windows I couldn't tell whether anyone was looking in—but I imagined a crowd while I writhed beneath his touch. I tilted my head back up and met his eyes with a girlish pout. The little lower lip tilt drove my husband wild. Only one secret weapon in our relationship and I pulled it out full throttle with no remorse. I wanted to put on a good show for the imaginary people behind the window, make 'em *ooo* and *ahh*.

"Sit up." The snap of his palm against my rib cage registered as pure sound before the bright pain tingled up my spine and made me bite my lip. "I'm going to fuck you. But not because you deserve it."

Max stepped out of the cage of my pants and pulled me until I sat up on the counter with a flinch whipping through my limbs. Every inch of me was tender, but I couldn't focus on the pain when his fingers skipped down his shirt and flicked open the button on his jeans. I trembled when he paused. One finger traced the line of his zipper—up and down—as if he was teasing his cock through the fabric, while also torturing me.

Each pull of the teeth as he lowered his zipper made me cringe. But he didn't move once he was done and made no attempt at pulling his hardness through the hole in his jeans.

He snatched my jaw with his clenched fingers until I flinched, my eyes half-closed with exhausted, humming bliss. Each second of pressure made my lips open without his command, until I had a less than subtle sense of what he was doing—and it was the perfect punishment.

"Stay."

When he walked over toward the back wall to get the step stool, I did my best to remain motionless. He would make it worse if I wiggled and got myself off by rubbing my slit against the shiny Formica. He dragged the stool in front of me. Each step he climbed on the ladder made his hard cock bob in front of me. I eased my tongue across my bruised lips. His glare was all the admonishment I needed—but there was more to come for my indiscretion.

"I didn't tell you to close your lips. Open up as wide as you can."

With his fingers clinging to the back of my hair driving me forward, he slid his cock down the back of my throat until I choked, any protests cut off with the pure bliss of his weight on my tongue. He moaned. The sound dove straight into my gut. I concentrated on keeping him in the back of my throat while my scalp pulsed from his unshakeable grip. When he pulled his hips back a fraction, then thrust back down, everything inside of me reflexively convulsed. My pussy walls clenched so hard it almost hurt. A strangled whimper leaked out of my full lips as I fought to take the fucking I'd begged for while his small movements pushed my naked ass in a jerky rhythm against the counter.

Quick little inhales of waffle batter and salty cock allowed me to take him deep, easing my tongue in mindless patterns against his dick's underside. His fingers trembled, but he didn't break his stride. I would be sore and begging for relief before Max emptied himself down the back of my throat. I had been too demanding—and this was my punishment, though it wasn't much of one when he pulled me so close that my forehead rested on his belly and his cock drove him into my forcibly relaxed muscles.

And then he slapped me. I hadn't been expecting the blow that landed across my cheek and sent my kinky meter soaring. All the while I struggled against his cock; the blow had squeezed my throat tight with arousal. A fresh sting lit up my nerve endings as I convulsed around him. When he did it again I knew to expect it. His palm made fresh contact on the other cheek. I fought not to jerk away as my whole mouth tightened. I swallowed him down again, oh so impossibly deep. I got the shocking, abrupt sting I craved, even as he pushed me past it to service him. I could tell from his body's soft, jerky tremor how much he was enjoying me.

We took on a cadence, a beat that shoved all my fears down low in my belly, allowing only the primal adventuress to come out and play, while my husband took what he needed and gave me everything he had in return. Even though I'd come to expect the blows—his roughness slamming down against my mouth, my ecstasy tangled with agony as my vision went white—my mind luxuriated in the pain, which bloomed like the red tinge I could only imagine flared across my cheeks. His hot cock bobbed in my mouth and made me blush as hard as the day we'd first met.

He made me remember our strength, our endurance and our light together. I knew no matter how far we took it back to the edge, we would always come back into that light. This pain was only a defiant flipped coin of pleasure; my naked flesh had so much more to look forward to with those hands he used to create an intricate multicolored travel guide to our life together, one as radiant and glowing as our wedding day. This was our version of TLC, a tenderness that made my cheeks ache with wanton, flushed heat, while my chest swelled with emotion and my eyes stung with tears. Our display was a true celebration of our years together, showing the whole town our twisted crazy love as it blazed through the windows.

When Max spilled down my throat, he tasted way better than any celebratory champagne.

A THOUSAND MILES APART

Tilly Hunter

I start by just teasing him, using my wand vibrator to come while he watches on the webcam, but forbidding him from wanking at the same time. He could be doing anything when the cam is off, in his little flat in Spain. But I don't think so—not when I get to see that desperate look in his eyes each evening. He struggles to even sit still. I find the best solution to that is to tell him to put his hands on his head like a naughty schoolboy. But even with him sitting still and me perching my laptop on a chair beside the bed, it takes a while for us to work out the screen logistics.

Tonight, I can see him from the knees up as he perches on the edge of his couch, body tense, arms raised. He's always naked before he turns the cam on. I can see his hard cock as I point my cunt at the camera at a slight angle so he can catch glimpses of it while I move the head of the wand around. Maybe I should have put him in a chastity device for the four months of his temporary assignment to Madrid. And kept the keys with me in England. But I think he would have exploded. Spontaneously combusted from the internal pressure. We're not into long-term orgasm denial. Sure, I make him wait a little. But I like it when he comes for me. Often.

So this enforced separation is an issue. Laurence has always said he'd go crazy without me. It's not just getting to come for me, it's the Friday night beatings with our favorite leather paddle and the way I tie him up and leave him to squirm. He calls it his weekend wind-down. All we can fit into this four-month stretch is one long weekend together, just over halfway in. Other than that it's all down to the webcam.

After two weeks of being forbidden to come, he tells me he's having trouble concentrating at work during the day. So I start ordering him to wank for me every night instead. Then I do some online shopping and put down his company apartment as the delivery address. I tell him not to open it until he's on the camera with me. The website assures me the package will arrive discreetly, but Laurence is still embarrassed when he finds the landlady of the block brandishing the brown box on the stairs. He says it rattles suspiciously. She apparently raised an eyebrow at him when she handed it over, but I bet that's just his overactive imagination.

I get him to remove all the packaging and lay everything out on the couch next to him. Two five-meter lengths of eight-millimeter black cotton rope. One set of steel handcuffs. One 1.75-inch ball gag. One medium-sized PVC butt plug in pink. One large bottle of lube. I almost ordered a blindfold but I need to see the look in his eyes, not just because his love to submit does things to my pussy, but to know that he's okay a thousand miles away from me.

Of course, when I get him to kneel on the couch and turn his ass to the camera so he can put the plug inside himself, I can't actually see his eyes. I see a close-up of his dark, puckered hole as he rubs lube all around it and pushes a slippery finger inside. He's already told me how much he misses my strap-on; it's seven and a bit inches long, 1.75 inches in girth, with a useful little curve to reach his prostate.

What surprises me is how much I miss my strap-on too. Most of our kink stems from his needs; in a way I'm the passive one doing what he asks. But as I see him bring the pink tip of the plug to his asshole, my view hemmed in by the edges of the screen, I desperately want to be there pressing my shiny purple dildo inside him with one long, slow thrust of my hips. The plug I've ordered him is only a cheap synthetic one. I've chosen things he won't need to pack for the flight home. They're a lot less luxurious than the collection we've built up at home, but it's a case of needs must.

"Do it slowly," I say. "I'm enjoying the view. I want you to take your time as you feel it stretching you wide." It's been well over a month since he had anything other than his own fingers up his ass, as far as I know. "That's it," I say into the computer. "Relax those muscles, open yourself up for me." I see his sphincter push out, sliding his flesh over the surface of the plug, and retract, pulling it back into him a little farther.

My skills at talking dirty have improved while he's been away. It's not something I'd thought much about before he left, but now our voices are our main point of contact.

I watch his hole close over the tapered stem of the plug like the hungry mouth of some fleshy, blind creature from a deep-sea trench. He's shaking a little as he turns back around and lowers his butt to the seat. He lets out a groan as he settles onto the velour cushion, his hands gripping the edge and arms tensed to ease the force of it pushing inside him.

"You feeling okay, honey?"

"Yes." It comes out as a low whisper that makes my pelvis tingle.

"Anything you want to ask me about the presents I got you?"

"Just the cuffs. How can I use those on myself? What if I can't get them open again?"

"It's all right," I tell him. "I tried it with our set here. As long as you make sure the keyholes are facing toward your hands. That's important so you can reach with the key."

"Okay."

He's very trusting. Personally, I'd be having a lot more doubts about the whole idea. But I'm telling the truth. I did try it at home and it is easily possible. I have to get everything in the right order next. And hope there's no emergency at his apartment block. I've actually thought through the possibilities. Fire, flood, earthquake. But I reckon the only tremors are going to be coming from Laurence shaking if he doesn't get to come.

"If you've no more questions then, I want you to put the gag in. And make sure you buckle it up tightly. I'll know if you don't."

I don't really know why I say this. I guess it's part of the façade of me being in charge and the possibility of him disobeying. God, how I'd love to spank his ass right now for an imaginary transgression. He was the one who first asked if we could get a gag for him. When we tried it out, he managed to form the word "tighter" around the rubber ball, albeit with deadened consonants.

He puts the black ball between his teeth and fiddles with the fastening. I see him cinch it so tight that the straps cut into the corners of his mouth. I've grown to love gagging him myself. I think it's the moment when he opens his mouth and lets me slide it in. It's another way of penetrating him, filling him all up. We once tried a little role-play where I was meant to be kidnapping and abusing him and he would pretend I was strong enough to do that. It didn't work because he didn't put up enough of a struggle. When I'd got him tied up and I waved the gag in front of his face menacingly, ready to force his mouth open, he practically lunged at it.

But seeing him do it to himself—that's new. That's something I'll be doing again when he gets home too. His thick fingers thread the buckle, bitten-down nails struggling to grip the end. I'm guessing the new leather is stiff, not like the supple, worn one we have at home, its strap so stretched we had to punch new holes in it. I wonder how the butt plug feels now that he's not using his arms to hold his weight off it.

"Now, I want you to put the handcuffs on, just like I said, with the keyholes facing out toward your hands. Not inward toward your body. Got it?"

"Uh-huh." He grunts his assent and picks up the cuffs, turning them the right way. He ratchets one closed around his left wrist. He looks up at the camera. A moment's hesitation, which is unusual for him, and I realize he's genuinely worried about this. It's not really the cuffs he should worry about though, it's the rope and the time it will take to undo that.

"Go on. It's all right, you'll be able to undo them easily. I know you want to feel that cold steel locking your wrists together, restraining you." Sometimes the things that sound sexy in the moment are ridiculous when you think back over it later. It doesn't matter. What matters is now and the way in which the words enhance the physical restriction, Laurence's mind making far more of it than it really is. More so than ever now, when he can literally get out of it himself without having to ask me to release him. He closes the cuff around his right wrist, then adjusts them both. A couple of clicks tighter. He looks up again for instructions. I see his Adam's apple bob as he swallows some saliva.

"Now I want you to take the keys and put them in the kitchen, next to the kettle. While you're there, get a glass from the cupboard." He likes clear instructions that leave no room for questions. But I can see questions in his eyes now and I wonder if I'm pushing him too far. We've been together eight years, married five. We're past the point of having to discuss every little thing we want to do beforehand. I know what he likes, what he definitely doesn't like, what he says he doesn't like but likes having forced on him. And the few funny little things that are a real no-no for him. It's been a long time since we experienced that lust-killing moment when he says "ouch" in the wrong way. But now I'm worried he's going to refuse, pull the gag out so he can say "no" with that tone of voice that makes my stomach turn to lead.

"It's only a few yards away," I say. "It's just psychological, having it in another room. I have everything planned. Will you do this for me?"

Everything planned. Right down to the fact that I wanted him to do handcuffs first, move keys after. He could, of course, have put the keys in another room before putting the cuffs on. Before the gag and plug even. But I'm playing my own game, having to persuade him without my physical presence. It'd be easier if I could just yank a handful of his hair or put my hand around his throat and tell him how I'm going to punish him for not complying immediately. I'm banking on the fact that he's far more likely to obey once he can feel that metal around his wrists. His mind won't be thinking entirely straight anymore. He'll want only to do as he's told, to suffer or enjoy as I order it.

He takes the keys off the couch, having to twist his whole body to turn to them, and gets up. I get a skewed close-up of his stiff dick as it passes across the screen diagonally. The sound of his bare feet on the carpet doesn't register on the mic. I've had him describe the apartment in detail so I know it has carpet in the little lounge, lino in the kitchen, cold terra-cotta tiles in the bathroom. I had him kneel on them to jerk off a few nights ago, the laptop set on a stand of tin cans.

He's back in moments, lifting the short chain between the cuffs over his cock as he sits down. I can see him edge it back toward his balls, shifting his legs apart.

"Stop that. We're not done yet. You have two lengths of rope to use." He freezes and looks at me. Wide-eyed and waiting. "I want you to tie your legs together, just above the knees. You know how—wrap it round a few times, then turn the rope and make a few passes between your legs to tighten it. You can make do with a reef knot this time."

He picks up one of the lengths of rope and shakes it out. Five meters is a bit excessive, but that's how it comes and I'm not going to faff about telling him to cut it and end up with fraying ends. It's actually quite difficult for him to tie with his hands together. He can't draw both ends round at the same time, so he lays a strand across one way, then takes the other end and passes it across in the opposite direction. It's a fumble to tighten them, but eventually he makes the turn and cinches the rope tight in the middle before tying it off. As he works the knot between his fingertips he lets out a little whimper of impatience.

"Now do the same for your ankles." Hesitation again, but it passes in a millisecond. I know the thoughts that went through his mind. Like, how long will it take him to undo both lots of rope on his legs so he can get to the keys to undo his wrists? But also, how many more days is it before I'm due to visit, when I've promised to hogtie him on the bathroom tiles? I wonder how the butt plug is feeling now, whether his muscles have accepted it or are still flexing and fluttering around the intrusion.

He turns slightly so he can straighten his legs out and bend forward to tie his ankles. All I get to see is the side of his head, with the leather strap of the gag pushing his fair hair out of place. He could do with a haircut. He turns back to me. He's all done. I wish I'd asked him to buy a couple of clothespins for those teeny man-nipples.

Now it's his turn to watch and wait. "Hands on your head again." The cuffs clank a little as he raises them.

I slowly undo my blouse and shrug it off my shoulders. I keep an eye on the little screen in the corner that shows me what he can see. I undress slowly to my underwear, then run my hands over my tits and down to my pussy. It feels daft, but I can tell he likes the show from the way his hips are rocking. He's probably trying to ease the tip of the plug onto that sweet spot in his ass that could make him come without laying a hand on his dick. "If you come before I give you permission, I'm going to order you a cock cage. I'll lock you into it when I come to see you and take the key home with me." That would give him six weeks of frustration, six weeks that would probably get him fired from work because his mind sure as hell wouldn't be on the job, and when you're supervising construction of a hydro-electric dam you really need to focus.

His rocking slows. I shrug off my bra and play with my nipples, making a few sound effects for his benefit. But stripping like this doesn't turn me on; I'd rather be naked as quickly as possible. What's turning me on right now is the little crease in Laurence's forehead as he fights the urge to pump his ass back against the plug. I slip my panties down, turning my butt in his direction a little so he gets a view of the curve of my ass as I bend. His breathing is getting loud now, a little moan with every exhalation.

I lie back on the bed, propped on an elbow so I can still see him, and move my fingers to my pussy. I want to do this by hand today. I don't want a machine blocking his view and I want to hear him come at the same time as me. I begin to circle my clit, drawing the wetness up from my vagina, playing two fingers just inside the entrance. I can see it in the corner of the screen at the same time as I can see Laurence thrust his hips a little before I catch his eye and he stops.

It will take me longer to come this way. So I make Laurence just sit and watch awhile as I gradually build up speed. I watch him as a little trickle of moisture escapes the corner of his mouth. He almost turns to wipe it on his inner arm but I give him a little shake of my head to let him know I'm still in charge. The sensation is gathering in my pelvis, my legs jerking a little wider.

"I want you to put some more lube on your hands and wank for me," I say. "I want you to come when I do. If you don't manage it, you'll have to wait until tomorrow." Will he get the timing right, reading my signs across a thousand miles? I'm not even sure he's left the lube where he can get to it and I realize my attention to detail has slipped. "When you come, I want you to do it into the glass."

He'd probably already guessed that was coming. What else would the glass be for?

He brings his arms down and reaches to the side. Thankfully, the lube is right there. He squirts some onto his hands and spreads it all around his fingers before taking hold of his dick. The cuffs allow him to swivel his wrist to move along its length while the fingers of his other hand straddle the base. He has to lean back into the couch cushions to gain full access, balls nestled in the tight space between his thighs.

Shots of adrenaline and god knows what other hormones are

careering round my pelvis now. My legs are pulsing wider open as the muscles of my butt clench. I slow my fingers. Although Laurence is under orders to come on my command, it's really up to me to make it happen; it's me who has to come at the right moment. I let him get in some mileage, pumping his uncut skin over the hardness beneath. He's rocking his hips at the same time, shifting the plug around in his ass.

He looks up at me and his breathing quickens. I use my other hand to stretch my labia apart, opening myself up for him to admire. It'll bring him to the point of coming. He stops a moment to reach for the glass and maneuver it in his free hand so the end of his dick points into it. He has to squirm his back up the couch from where he's slid down so he can angle it right.

"You'd better slow down," I say, "I'm not ready." He groans, but slows his hand. I'm just teasing him; I have to slow down too or I'll prove myself a liar. I circle my clit at a measured pace, keeping it on the edge. Then I go for it. "I'm going to come. Wait...wait...now."

It's good to have a nonmechanical orgasm for once. I have to make a real effort to keep my fingers moving and wring every ounce from it. It's the opposite of the wand, where you have to move your fingers to switch it off, not to keep it going. Laurence groans low and long, teeth clenched around the gag, as he spurts into the glass.

When I recover enough to look up at the screen, he's sat upright once more and looking at me for further instructions. He knows what I'm going to say, but he wouldn't presume to act without orders. Or perhaps he thinks I'm going to tell him to store the spunk in the fridge so he can drink it cold. Or top it up every day until he reaches a glassful. It's an idea, but for now I want to see him bring that glass to his lips and tip the milky fluid down his throat.

"Take the gag off and drink it."

It's funny how a spurting penis looks like it's spewing out pints of the stuff, but actually one load of his spunk barely covers the bottom of the glass. He has to tip it up and wait as it runs down the side before he has a mouthful worth swallowing. Then he sticks his tongue in the glass as deep as he can get it and slurps the dregs. The sight of that makes me almost ready to go again. I consider using the wand before I go to sleep.

"Thank you, darling," he says and I smile. I'm not even there. And I can't hold him while he relaxes in his restraints with the taste of his own spunk on his tongue.

"How was work?" We talk about our days. The little annoyances of work, the weather (hot for him, rainy for me), our plans for the weekend.

"You'd better undo everything before I sign off," I say. "Just to make sure."

"I suppose so," he says. "But I'm comfy like this. I can't wait to see you."

"I know. Fifty-one days to go."

SWITCH

Mina Murray

B y the time Grady tells me what he's going to do to me, I'm
naked, blindfolded and not inclined to argue. We haven't
seen each other in weeks, a consequence of my own erratic
schedule and the frequent trips he has to take for work.

It's not like we've been out of touch the whole time, though.
Whenever he's away, Grady calls me twice a week. Normally I
hate talking on the phone, but with him it's different. Especially
on Friday nights, when we pour our filthy hearts out to each other
and he convinces me, time and again, that he's king of the mind-
fuck. His teasing voice ties me up in knots and I end up admit-
ting things I never would have dared if we'd been chatting over
Skype, or in the flesh. I think he knows it, too, understanding
the difference distance can make, the false sense of safety it gives
you. And the dirty stories he spins for me! Of erotic tortures;
of lust denied; of virtue punished and vice rewarded...Grady's
twisted imagination easily equals, if not outstrips, my own.

So when he turns up on my doorstep a full week ahead of

schedule, with an overnight bag and a glint in his eye, I almost cream myself.

"You're early!"

I don't mean to sound accusatory, but I've been practicing a new dance routine and am not exactly dressed for a sexy reunion. The yoga pants I'm wearing have bleach stains around the hems, and my tank top has also seen better days.

"Yeah? Well, you're sweaty," he says, and drops his bag in the hall.

"Sorry," I say, grimacing. "Let me take a quick shower and I'll welcome you properly."

Grady kicks the door shut behind him and tugs me into an embrace.

"I'm just teasing, Cass," he murmurs against my throat. "You smell amazing. You smell like *woman*."

I groan at that. He always knows the right things to say, the things that get me wet.

Strong hands grip my hips and heft me up against the wall. I have no choice but to wrap my legs around his waist, unless I want to fall. My arms loop around his neck and I lean in for a kiss, but he holds himself just out of reach.

"I missed you," he says.

"Oh baby, I know," I purr, and rub myself against him. "I missed you, too."

He lets me kiss him then, light brushes of my lips against his that gradually build into something deeper and more consuming. It's been so long, I feel like I could almost come from this alone: from his tongue in my mouth, his breathless kiss, the pressure of his hips rocking against me. But it's not enough, and eventually we have to break for air.

I unravel myself from around him. Even before my bare feet touch the floorboards, I'm reaching for his belt.

"Not yet." He stills my hand. "Not till after I give you your present."

"Grady, you shouldn't have."

"It's something we'll both enjoy."

He smiles, a sly look that does nothing to warm his eyes. That's when I start to get nervous.

See, Grady has this uncanny ability to change gears, right when I least expect it. One minute he'll be all sweet and solicitous, then some hidden switch will trip inside him and he'll become this domineering bastard who'll make me crawl to him, make me beg. He'll drag me to my limits and then make *me* take that final step into the void, alone—and fully conscious of what I'm doing. And when I'm on the other side—after I've fallen—he'll praise me and tell me he's proud of me, and that's what will make me cry.

Sometimes I don't know which version of Grady I love more. But I know which one I'm getting this afternoon.

"It's something we talked about, over the phone," he says, as if that's going to help me narrow it down. We talked about a lot of things, in our late-night exchanges. I *said* a lot of things.

"But you have to close your eyes. Promise?"

I feel the sudden urge to cross my fingers behind my back.

"I promise."

Grady searches my face, to make sure I'm telling the truth. Not that I'm a hard make. I've never been a very good liar. I always have a tell.

"See, you say that now," Grady notes, "but you've cheated in the past. Haven't you, pet?"

"Yes, Grady," I whisper, staring at his boots.

"Well, that's why I brought this."

He pulls a blindfold out of his back pocket and holds it up for me to inspect. It's black and it's leather, heavy-duty enough to keep out the light, soft enough to mold to my features. Which it does, when Grady slips it gently over my head and pulls the straps taut.

"Now, that's better, isn't it? No need to worry that you'll peek, by accident, and break your word."

He's right, of course. I would have peeked. I've never been good at delayed gratification. Which is why it's so hard to stand still and wait for his next move.

Without my sight, every sound is amplified, from the birds in the tree outside to the scraping sound of Grady's bag being lifted from the floor.

Grady takes my hand in his.

"Wh-where are we going?"

Surely he won't lead me outside like this, blindfolded and dressed as I am?

"Relax," he soothes, "we're not leaving the house."

"Then why do you need your bag?"

"You ask too many questions."

And that's the end of the discussion. He starts walking, not in a straight line, but in a weaving sort of dance, pulling me behind him like a marionette. He leads me in and out of more rooms than I thought my small house possessed, but that's probably just the darkness screwing with my senses. Either that or he's doubling back deliberately, just to destabilize and disorient me. It's working.

"Here we are."

Grady urges me forward, his hand in the small of my back. The sudden movement takes me off guard and I stumble, bumping into something cold and unyielding. Even though Grady grabs my elbow to steady me, I still fling my hands out blindly, scared of falling.

"Hey, you're okay. I've got you," he says. "We're in the study.

You just ran into the radiator."

It figures. I did the same thing earlier this week, only I wasn't blindfolded then, so had no excuse. When he's certain I've got my balance back, he lets go of my elbow. There's a thunk when he sets his bag down again.

A few moments pass during which there's no noise, other than our quiet breathing. The anxiety builds, and I can't suppress it, no matter how many times I remind myself that I trust Grady, that he's never asked more than I can give.

When he finally speaks, his voice sounds abnormally loud.

"Take your clothes off. Strip for me."

I start turning around, ready to give him a show, but he corrects me quickly.

"No, Cass. Face forward."

Face the window, is what he means. Face the tall, wide window that looks out onto the back garden. There's a fence between my property and the house behind mine, but it's not very high. I hesitate.

"Are you resisting me already?"

"No, Grady."

"Then take your top off. Slide the straps off your shoulders, roll the top down over your hips and let it fall to the ground."

I do as he says.

"Good. Now the bra, as well."

If the neighbors are home, and snooping...well, I've just given them an eyeful of tit.

"But you can't see me like this," I say petulantly.

"I can see you fine. The glass reflects you beautifully. Now quit arguing and take off those pants."

In the spirit of his order, I should probably remove my panties as well. But I exercise a small act of defiance and leave them on.

"Pretty," Grady says, plucking at them. They're nothing

special, just white cotton printed with tiny blue flowers. He's probably amused at how virginal they look. "But I want you bare."

My hands tremble as I tug the fabric down. It's a ridiculous response—I've stripped for him before, and I'm not shy about my body. But there's something about this time that's more titillating than usual. Maybe it's because I can't see him, but he can see me, and it puts me at such a disadvantage. Maybe it's because I wouldn't be able to tell if someone was watching from the other side of the glass. Would Grady call an end to the proceedings if there *was* actually someone out there? As well as I know him, I can't answer that question. Not that I have much time to ponder it.

He nudges me forward, until the radiator is pressed hard up against my knees. I whimper as his fingers delve between my legs, testing how aroused I am. It's an effort to accept what I'm given and not demand more.

"You've been such a good girl," he says, "I think you've earned your present."

He steps away from me. Seconds later I hear rummaging. He's retrieving something from his bag. My pulse quickens when I hear a silvery liquid spill of a sound, a sound that can mean only one thing.

"Do you know what I'm holding?" Grady asks. "You do, don't you?"

I nod.

"Say it."

I can only manage a whisper.

"Chains."

"That's right," he says, his breath hot against my neck. "I had them made especially for you. With padded cuffs, to protect that creamy-soft skin of yours. See how much I love you?"

He slings the chains around my shoulders and laughs when I jump.

"Cold, are we?"

No, just edgy.

"A bit."

"Don't worry. I'll warm you up soon enough."

He must be undressing now. I mentally catalogue each rustle and match it to the garment he's shedding.

Before I'm done visualizing the slow revelation of his naked form, it's pressed up against me. Grady is clearly excited by this scenario. He grabs my ass and squeezes. I arch my back, and he presses his erection between my buttocks. He starts thrusting gently, as he describes what he's going to do to me.

"I'm going to bend you over," he threatens. "I'm going to cuff your wrists and your ankles, chain you to the radiator so you can't get away, and then I'm going to fuck you, right in front of this window."

Oh god *yes*.

"Promise?"

His reply takes the form of a strong hand between my shoulder blades, pushing me down until my cheek rests against the cushion of the window seat. The chains slide off my shoulders and clink against the panes.

"Well look at that," Grady drawls, "pretty in pink."

I love the way he talks, crude and elegant at the same time. I love the way he objectifies me, like he's doing now, on his knees and spreading my legs wide so he can look his fill. His tongue flickers over my secret flesh and I cry out, it's so good. These weeks apart have felt like an eternity.

I'm hoping Grady forgets the chains that little bit longer, long enough to make me come, but he's far too clever for that.

Before I know it, my ankles are cuffed as well and he's telling me to stretch my arms out some more. He wants me restrained, yes, but he also wants me comfortable. He secures the chains around the radiator and makes swift work of the wrist cuffs. When he's done, there's enough play in the metal lengths for me to slightly adjust the position of my hands if I need to, but not to do anything else. Except wait, that is.

"You look so good like this," Grady says. He rubs his cock along my folds, slick with desire for him, then enters me with a groan. "My beautiful captive."

The way he has me bound, the precise angle, opens me up for him like never before, and I'm trapped not just by the chains, but by my own pleasure.

"Grab my waist," I plead, "work me back onto you."

And he does, even though I'm not in a position to be giving orders.

I wish I had a hand free to play with my clit, but all I can do is clench and unclench my fists in time with Grady's thrusts. I can't even grind against anything. The top of the radiator is too low, and wouldn't really work anyway (wrong shape). The edge of the cushion is too far away, and the slack in the chain won't stretch that far. The ankle cuffs hold my legs securely apart, so any friction I could create by closing them is denied me. I try contracting the muscles around my bud, and that feels good, but isn't going to get me where I need to go. Grady senses my distress. He reaches down, curves his palm over my mound, and oh, it's beautiful.

"Th-thank you," I stutter.

"Just keep doing that clenching thing you were doing," he pants. "Ah *fuck*, yeah—that."

My pleasure unfurls like a tight green bloom, and I'm on the verge of the most blissful orgasm ever when he suddenly says,

"Ow, ow, ow," and pulls out of me.

"What are you doing, what's wrong?"

"Leg cramp, real bad. Gotta stretch it out."

This is the second time today he's left me teetering on the edge of release. I know this time it's not his fault, but it's still not fair. *I've been good*, I want to scream, after a few minutes have passed. *I deserve a reward.*

"Sorry, Cass," Grady calls from the kitchen. "I'm better now, just getting some water." The fridge door opens and closes. Footsteps pad back toward me. Finally.

If I was expecting Grady to pick up right where he left off, well, I was mistaken. It's as if the clock has reset, and we're starting now from the beginning. He runs a hand over my ass, kisses the nape of my neck, performs other preparatory gestures that I don't really need.

"Please," I beg, "*please.*"

He takes the hint.

But this isn't the way Grady fucked me before. In fact, everything about this is different. From the way he enters me, butting insistently with that broad, blunt head, to the swiveling pattern of his strokes, to the way he stretches me.

And then I recall that fantasy I'd confessed one night, when I drunk-dialed Grady, and everything makes sense. Just as I can frame the thought, *Oh fuck, I'm getting screwed by a stranger*, there's a tap at the windowpane. An unseen hand removes my blindfold and all my suspicions are confirmed.

A bolt of fear streaks through me when I see Grady standing outside, fully dressed. Guilt and lust war across his face as he watches his best friend moving inside me. Because that's whose image is reflected in the glass. Stephen. Who is tall and dark and gorgeous. Who had coffee with me yesterday. Who gave me absolutely no warning about what Grady was planning. I guess that's the thing about a switch fantasy though—it loses its power if you know it's coming.

"Hey beautiful," Stephen says tentatively, unsure of my reaction.

"You sons of bitches!" I yell. Then I try to push myself back onto him, eager to cram as much of him inside me as I can. Which is a challenge, and not just because my range of motion is restricted.

The rich baritone of his laugh rumbles through me, and he flexes forward to throw open the window. The breeze curls around my waist, then down between my legs, a shock of cold to that hot, hot place.

"Go on, say it again. I don't think Grady heard you the first time."

I'm more than happy to repeat myself.

"Grady," I gasp, as Stephen drives into me, "you fucker, you sneaky son of a bitch..."

My boyfriend is currently perched on the edge of the window, half in and half out of the house.

"Do you like your present, sweetheart?"

I should be angry at him, or at least pretend to be, but I just can't. Because there's no way I can disguise how much I'm enjoying this. All of it. Grady's surprise visit. The teasing. The chains. The perfect realization of one of my deepest desires.

"Yes," I cry. "Yes, yes, *yes!*"

Grady flashes a look at Stephen, a look so triumphant, so full of heat, that it makes me wonder just how deep their friendship goes.

And then Grady's hand slides between my legs, and his fingers tweak my clit, and I can't think at all.

"Don't close your eyes when you come," he says. And I know it's absurd, considering everything that's happened so far, but *that's* the request that almost breaks me.

When I start to protest, Grady cups my chin in his free hand and tilts my face up toward his.

"No arguments, Cassandra."

Oh god, that voice. Like a velvet lash against my skin.

The orgasm builds in me the way a storm does, clouds gathering from the four corners of my body to circle darkly around my core. And then it's on me, and I'm coming, holding Grady's gaze as I contract around his best friend's cock. *This is wrong*, I think. *It's wrong. But that just makes it better.*

"Jesus, Grady," Stephen exclaims, "is she always this tight?"

"Yep," he replies, still stroking me.

I can't believe the way they're talking about me, in the third person, as if I'm an object, as if I'm not even here. But I'd be lying if I said it didn't flick my switch. A long, low moan works itself from my throat. I think I'm going to come again.

"Aw *fuck*," Stephen shouts, as I clutch around him. He shoves into me desperately, determined not to be left behind. His final, frenzied motions spin out my pleasure, until my body has nothing left to give.

When I slump forward, he leaps into action, unchaining me, loosening my cuffs.

Grady crawls onto the window seat and settles me into his lap.

"You were magnificent," he says, then kisses me fiercely.

"And what about me?" Stephen asks, with a smile. He's still holding my chains. They're wrapped around his forearm, the metal gleaming bright against his dark skin.

"You were magnificent, too," Grady says.

And just when I think the day holds no more surprises, he leans across my body and kisses his friend on the mouth. Hard.

When he breaks away, Stephen looks dazed. I know how he feels.

Grady holds out his hand for my chains. I can tell Stephen doesn't want to give them up, but he does.

"Come on, Cass," Grady says, "let's go upstairs."

My legs are a little shaky, so I lean on him for support. We're almost halfway up the stairs when he slows his pace.

"Are you coming, Stephen?"

"Right behind you, buddy."

Grady stumbles at that, and his misstep tells me everything I need to know.

"Careful," Stephen says, then reaches out to steady his friend. His big hand grips Grady by the scruff of his neck. His shadow looms over us—me and Grady both—and I know for sure that the day's not over yet.

THE BIRDS
AND THE BEES

Giselle Renarde

W here are you going with that thing?"

Becky jumped out of her sandals. "Jesus Christ, Walker! Give me a heart attack, why don't you?"

He watched from across the room, grinning as she leaned against the balcony door. "Planning to put on a show for the neighborhood?"

"Who, me? No." Her heart fluttered as she tightened her grip on the vibrator. "No, it's really stupid. You're gonna laugh."

Walker crossed his arms in front of his chest. "Try me."

"Come on, then." She slipped her sandals back on her feet and opened the screen door.

Last week's heat wave had broken, and a lovely breeze cut through the summer's warmth. Sunshine danced across Becky's bare arms and legs as she held her battery-powered vibe against her chest.

Walker teased her herbs with his fingers, like he was petting a cat. "So this is what you get up to when say you're out here gardening."

"No!" She giggled, backing up past the patio table, until the tomato plants tickled her legs. Lowering her voice, she said, "I didn't bring the vibe out here to use on *me*. It's for the tomatoes, I swear!"

"Is that right?" Walker raised an eyebrow, like he didn't believe her. Well, of course he didn't believe her. If she didn't know it was the truth, she wouldn't have believed herself.

"I'm serious. Look at these tomato plants."

He nodded, mock sympathetically. "Yeah, they look like they could use a good fuck."

"Stop laughing at me!" But she was laughing at herself, so who was she to judge? "Listen, we've got these big-ass tomato plants with these pretty yellow blossoms, but what happens? The blossoms wither and die and fall off. No tomatoes. Big, beautiful plants and not a single fruit."

"Vegetable."

"Fruit," she said. "The tomato is the fruit of a vegetable plant."

"Okay, Dr. Know-It-All." He grabbed the vibe from her hand and hid it behind his back. "So tell me what the dildo's for."

Her cheeks felt hot, and it wasn't just the sun. "Well, I read online that tomato blossoms need bees to land on them. The buzzing helps with pollination, somehow."

"So you thought you'd come out here and help Mother Nature along?"

Walker slid the vibe out from behind his back, holding it by the base. It was pretty sexy, watching a big strong man grip a dildo like that. When he started whacking it against his palm, the way he would with a crop or a switch or a wooden spoon, Becky got shivers.

"I want fresh tomatoes," she said. "Don't you?"

"Tomatoes I can take or leave." Grabbing her hips, he spun

her around. When his forearm found the base of her ribs, he pulled her so close the curve of her ass filled the saddle of his hips. "It's you I'm more interested in."

"Walker!" She struggled halfheartedly. "What are you doing? Anyone could look up and see us."

"See what?" His breath fell hot on her ear. "See a man taking a woman in his arms? Or see a damsel struggling against a villain?"

He was right. She'd attract more attention wiggling around than she would standing still.

"Anyway," he went on, "who's really gonna see us, up this high?"

"Neighbors could, if they came out on their balconies."

"Not with all your grapevines growing up the trellis. Who's gonna see through that?" Holding the vibrator in front of her with the cock end facing down, he said, "Turn me on."

"What are you doing? Put that away." She pressed on his wrist, but he was too strong. "Come on. You'll get us arrested for indecent exposure."

"Exposure? What's exposed? We're both fully dressed."

"Yeah, but...but..." She tried to steal the dildo from his hand, but he maintained such a tight grip that it wouldn't budge. She pushed on his arm with both hands, writhing against the one that held her in place. No luck. Stuck.

"Somebody's getting a little too fidgety for my liking. Open up."

Becky did as she was told, opening her mouth without knowing what he planned to do.

She should have known he'd cram the fake cock between her lips, sideways, and say, "Here, hold this for a second."

Biting into the vibrator's rubbery plastic casing, she kept its shaft between her lips while Walker rifled through her bag of gardening implements—gloves, trowels, old nylons for tying tomato plants to their stakes.

"What, no twine?" he asked.

She whimpered because—ouch! Twine would dig into her tender flesh, cutting her wrists to bits. And it was in there, too, hanging right out the front pocket.

But Walker was only teasing, getting her heart rate up, giving her something to panic about. Lifting a pair of nylons from the bag, he said, "I guess these'll have to do."

God, Becky hoped nobody could see her like this, standing on the balcony with a dildo between her teeth while a beastly man tied her hands behind her back.

"That's more like it." He stole the vibrator from her mouth and used it to spank her thigh. Saliva from her tongue smacked her bare skin, accentuating the ruthless clout. Not that it *hurt*. It didn't, not really, but it spoke of things to come.

Digging his fingers into her shoulder, he said, "I love the way your chest sticks out when I bind you up like this. You must be so turned on—look how hard your tits are."

Reaching under the fabric of her airy sundress, he found her braless breasts and squeezed.

"Oh god." Becky's knees buckled. If it wasn't for Walker's big hand on her chest, she'd have fallen right over. "Please..."

"Please *what*?" Walker asked, in a way that sounded exceedingly self-satisfied.

"Please," she said, "turn on the vibe."

She wasn't wearing a bra—never did, at home in the summertime—but she *was* wearing panties. Could Walker find his way beyond them? There wasn't much she could do, with her hands tied behind her back.

"How high should I set it?" Hooking his chin over her shoulder, he held the vibe with one hand, wrapping his fist around the shaft. No fear. With the other hand, he turned the base, bringing it to life. "Low, maybe?"

She watched as the familiar cock fell between her thighs, over her sundress. He didn't even try to go underneath, just pressed the dildo against her mound, stroking slowly, lifting the fabric until the short skirt revealed even more flesh.

Becky's heart raced, more from her feeling of exposure than from the actual vibrations. In fact, with the setting on low, she could barely feel it. She looked in every direction, up through the wide-leafed vines at the neighbors' empty balconies, and then down to the street where cars drove by and pedestrians carried grocery bags down the sidewalk. All that life, and nobody looked up. Nobody noticed that she'd been bound, or that Walker was holding a dildo between her legs.

His chin remained hooked over her shoulder, his face so close that his stubble pricked her cheek. That was such a great sensation, getting stabbed by facial hair. Made her feel raw, frenzied, swollen. Her clit throbbed inside a prison of cotton. If only Walker would catch the elastic waistband with his thumbs and push them down to her knees. She wanted to feel the vibe closer to her flesh.

"Please," Becky whispered, afraid the neighbors might hear. "Could you turn it up to medium?"

"Medium?" Walker whacked her cunt with the vibe. Her clit really must have become distended in that short time, because she felt the dildo slap like a bolt of lightning down her thighs. "Low's not good enough, huh?"

"No," she moaned.

"You want more?"

"Yes..."

"I can't hear you." He traced the vibe across her lips, and a gush of saliva flooded her tongue. "Speak up."

"I want more," she said with conviction. "Turn it up."

Walker rolled the base to its next setting, and the buzzing got louder, higher in pitch. He traced the vibe down her neck as she kept an eagle eye on the adjacent balconies. If one of the neighbors stepped outside, she'd flip. Where could she hide?

"Relax," Walker said, right in her ear. "We'll never get you off until you calm yourself down."

"Ohhh..."

The dildo teased her tits, drawing them into tighter buds as he moved from one to the other. There was a definite difference between low and medium.

"Between my legs," Becky said. "Please?"

"Where?" He traced the buzzing cock down her belly.

"Between my legs." She swallowed desperately. "Do my clit."

"Your clit?" he asked, so loudly she cringed in his arms.

"Please stop teasing me." She would have taken matters into her own hands if she had access to them. "Just do it."

"Do this?" He launched the dildo between her slightly open legs, slapping her cunt with the thing and then holding it there. "Close your eyes."

"No."

"Do it."

"I can't."

"You can."

Becky took a deep breath, barely feeling the buzz against her pussy. This was a show of trust. She had to trust that he'd play lookout even as he toyed with her clit. Could she trust him that much?

Nothing had changed since they'd come out here. No neighbors on their balconies. No drivers or pedestrians looking up. She was safe in Walker's care. She closed her eyes.

All at once, vibrations soared through her, sparkling in her veins like soda water. The pulse centered in her clit, of course, but she felt it everywhere. "Oh my god."

"Ride it," Walker said, catching the dildo on her dress as he pressed it between her legs.

She straddled the vibe like a broomstick, rocking on it, feeling it buzz against her panties and her dress. Her cunt felt so enclosed under those layers. Her panties felt tighter by the moment, the elastic edges digging into her skin as she moved on the vibe.

"Tell me how good it feels." Walker's gritty voice was tinged with desperation now. "Come on. I want to hear how much you love it."

Her clit throbbed within the confines of her compressed pussy lips. Her juices had nowhere to go—they were trapped within her folds, barely spilling out onto the crotch of her cotton underwear. Had these panties always been so tight?

"Turn it up," she pleaded.

"Not until you tell me how much you love it."

"Enough that I want to come, even though someone might hear. Enough that I'm not struggling anymore. I'm not fighting you. Doesn't that say it all?"

"I suppose it does."

Without pulling the cock out from between Becky's locked thighs, Walker spun the dial, releasing the full rage of her vibrator's prowess. It worked so hard it rattled, but its efforts paid off. Becky's insides clenched as an inner buzz echoed the outer one. Her clit throbbed between her slick pussy lips. She rode the cock, but just barely. She was too afraid that any sudden movements would frighten her orgasm away. And now that she'd come so close, she really wanted to get off.

"Becky," Walker whispered, "open your eyes. We've got company."

Her heart nearly stopped as her lids flew open. Their company wasn't human, though. The only prying eyes belonged to a sparrow nestled neatly on the trellis. Cocking its tiny head, it watched them curiously. Becky couldn't stop smiling. It was so cute, so tiny and darling with its little brown beak and its gleaming gaze.

The raging dildo pounded a percussive beat against Becky's mound, but she bit her lip to keep quiet. She could feel the buzz in her nipples, and when Walker pinched there, she felt it in her clit. Oh god, this was it. Her orgasm crashed like an ocean wave, nearly toppling her over. She didn't want to scare the bird, but how could she possibly stay quiet?

"Walker..."

"Shh-shh-shh!"

"No, I can't." She folded in on herself, frightening the sparrow away but drawing Walker with her. His chest pressed against her back and her arms as they both went down.

With the dildo lodged between her thighs, Becky met the balcony's base. As her knees found the unforgiving concrete, she remained locked in his full-bodied grip, coming hard, trying not to make a sound but whimpering and moaning—and laughing, when she thought about the sparrow that had wisely flown the coop.

"Enough," she said, as pleasure spun into pain. "Too much. I can't...I can't..."

She couldn't even speak, just pant and gasp and suck in the biggest breaths she could manage.

Walker tried to pull the dildo from between her locked thighs, but it stayed there, sticking up like a battery-powered erection. Holding her from behind, he spun the dial from high to medium to low to off.

They rested together as the summer sun painted the leafy

garden a vibrant shade of green. All Becky could smell was that characteristic aroma of tomato plants, coupled with the musky odor of Walker's skin. As they breathed together, he kissed her hair. They were quiet, but the city made noises: skateboards and buses and car horns and construction. Birds, but no bees.

"What now?" Becky asked as Walker pulled the vibrator from between her thighs.

Turning it on again, he pressed the head to one of the tomato plants' tiny yellow blossoms. "We'll start them out on low..."

POTLUCK

Alva Rose

It was our turn to host Sunday night potluck, and Manuel had been in a cleaning frenzy all day. The kitchen, dining room, living room and bathroom were all spotless, and he'd moved on to the completely unnecessary task of cleaning our bedroom. I was a little put out that he was so preoccupied with cleaning that he'd failed to notice—or consciously ignored—all my attempts at affection. Sundays are practically made for languorous hours in bed, for sleepy, drawn-out foreplay and exploring the erotic potential of some underappreciated square inch of the body—the back of the knee, the curve of the calf, the crown of the head. Manuel's cleaning frenzy approached blasphemy. *Maybe I'll give it one more shot*, I thought, creeping into the bedroom to check in on his frantic tidying. *For his own good.* I stood in the doorway, cleared my throat, smiled at him, reached out for him when he whizzed by me, tried to strike up a conversation, but did not receive so much as a word in response.

"Baby," I grumbled, crossing my arms, "nobody's going to see the bedroom. It isn't even messy..."

"Well, it doesn't hurt to clean anyway!" he snapped, looking over his shoulder as he shut the closet door.

After five years together, three under the same roof, I should have known better than to try reasoning with him. Manuel was fully aware of how silly it was to sweat over the cleanliness of our bedroom, but couldn't stop himself from reaching for something beyond perfection. The studio we had previously occupied was far too small for company, but when it came to those weekly potlucks among our friends, we made up for it by always bringing plenty of food and booze, then insisting that the rotating hosts leave the post-dinner cleanup to us. We were an exception to the rule that everyone took turns hosting, and at some point, it became a running joke that Steven and Manuel must be homeless, or hoarders, and very good at hiding it. When we moved into a spacious two-bedroom, Manuel was eager to show off our new digs, but as always, the thought of not making an excellent impression was driving him up the wall.

He whipped the rag out of his back pocket and stood on his tiptoes to dust—of all the silly things—the top of the closet door frame. Wordlessly, I walked up behind him and placed my hands on his waist. "Come on, babe, come sit with me for a minute..."

"Steven," he warned firmly, still slapping the rag over the beveled molding.

I wrapped one arm around him and raised my free hand to hold his wrist still. "Hey, just give me ten seconds. Shhh." He struggled for a second then huffed and stood there tapping his foot. "Just stand still for ten seconds," I demanded. "Just stand here with me, and breathe..." He exhaled slowly, trying to humor me, and soon relaxed into my embrace. His head fell back, and I could see everything in his body going tense, then releasing. "You nervous?" I asked, quietly.

"Of course I am," he sighed.

"I know." I kissed the top of his head and held him tighter. "You should take a little breather before people start showing up."

Manuel shrunk in my arms and turned around. "Okay. For you, I will." Was he kidding? I wasn't sure. But I knew if he just gave himself time to relax, he'd feel better. If he was doing it to appease me, so be it.

"Always the people pleaser, eh?" I let go of his wrist and kissed his nose, which always made him melt and blush. This time was no different, and he hummed and shut his eyes, locking his hands at the back of my neck. "The house looks great," I assured him.

"I kno-ooow," he moaned.

"And in a few hours you'll forget you ever worried about this anyway."

"I know."

I had nothing left to say, satisfied with his willingness to at least pay attention to me instead of the dust in our bedroom, so I waited until I caught his brown eyes in mine, steeled my gaze and shifted my hand to his neck. With a strong note of roughness, tinged with great care, I held him by the throat and kissed his tight mouth, which immediately yielded under my touch. Manuel moaned softly and pressed his body to mine, my arm going a little tighter around his back. His lips parted conspicuously, begging for my tongue, but I pulled away, to pathetic squeals of protest. "Hmm, you seem pretty relaxed now," I teased, cocking an eyebrow, my mind already concocting a plan of attack.

Manuel snickered and turned his face away from me,

mumbling, "You started it!" He moved to push past me, his cheeks reddening, but I stood my ground. Again I grabbed his neck and turned him back to me, giving him the deep, lewd kiss he'd been asking for just seconds prior. He gasped and submitted himself to my attentions for just a moment before he moaned, "Steven, it's almost seven already! We can't!"

"Almost seven?" I countered, snatching the rag that still dangled from his right hand. His eyes were wide open as I shoved his back against the closet door and pushed his arms up over his head. "It's six fifty. And you know *damn well* our friends aren't showing up before seven fifteen." I leaned against him, my hips pressing into his abs, and swiftly wrapped the rag around both of his wrists and then the metal coat hook that hung over the door. I pulled it into a snug, bulky knot, and concluded, "They *never* do."

I had to make quick work of him, as enough struggling would surely undo the knot. If he were half an inch taller, he might have been able to pull it up and off the hook. But he isn't that tall, so with his arms stretched up as they were, his shirt lifted enough to show off the dark triangle of hair that began in a point at his navel, then spread and disappeared under the waistband of his tight gray boxer-briefs. "Steven!" he shrieked, failing to hide a smile. "What if someone is on time this week?"

I shook my head, planted my lips on his neck and felt him swallowing. I raised my mouth to his ear and answered, "Then I'll just have to let you go, huh?" One of my hands dropped down to his crotch and felt for stiffness behind the worn, blue denim. "Do you want me to stop?" I asked, stroking him through his jeans.

By way of answer, he whined and pushed against my hand. He couldn't bring himself to say no—clearly he wanted it to go on—or yes—then he'd have to admit that he had forgotten why there was even a rag handy in the first place. "Come on, babe," I whispered, burying my fingers in his dark, curly hair and tugging for emphasis, "Tell me you want it."

"Yes," he squeaked out, grinding against my hand. "I want it..."

"Mmm, that's better." I kept him pushed against the door with my body as my hands went to work on his belt, button and zipper. Once that was done, I growled and fanned out my fingers on his lower back, pushing them under his clothes. If only I'd had time, I might have been spreading those soft cheeks and plunging my cock between them, one hand around his neck and one on his member. I would have had time, if he hadn't been cleaning all day. As if in punishment, I tugged his pants down and delivered a hard, full-hand smack.

"Oh!" Manuel squirmed and pushed his hips out; I felt his throbbing cock poking my thigh. I couldn't wait any longer and wrapped my hand around its base, working my loose fingers up and down the shaft. He turned his face upward and searched for my lips. I obliged, gripping the base of his jaw and dominating his mouth with mine. Manuel's breath escaped him in long sighs, his tongue and lips urgent in their movements, perhaps attempting to make up for his relative immobility. The door clattered in its frame as he twisted and turned, impatient for me to do more, and soon I broke away from his mouth and with one last look at his eager face, dropped to my knees.

I opened my mouth wide with my tongue flat and held the tip of my man's cock on its warm, slick surface, sliding flesh against flesh. I pushed farther and farther down the shaft, retreating only to advance down its length again, and heard a restrained moan from above. I closed my lips and slowly pulled them back, my tongue dancing on the bulge and playing his thin sheath back and forth. His voice newly deep with arousal, Manuel growled, "O-ohh, fuck..." He was near-imperceptibly trying to pump his cock between my lips, but I wouldn't have it, not yet.

Kissing just the head of his pulsing tool, I stared up at him with deceptively sweet, sleepy eyes, moaning my enjoyment with a long, low, "Mmmmmm..." He looked down at me, his face reading desperation, lust and affection, and I wrapped my hands around the backs of his thighs, my fingers tightening until he tensed beneath them, thrusting forward. I let go with one hand and slammed my palm into his ass again.

The sharp clap and his choked moan met my ears and I pushed farther down his length, alternately squeezing and caressing where I'd hit him. I delivered another blow, clutching his other cheek with ruthless, gruff fingers, and Manuel cried out, shaking. I retreated off his cock and grabbed it, pointing its head toward the ceiling, and ran my tongue up the underside, lingering on its apex, then steadily took it all in my mouth and throat. I closed my lips tight at its root, sucked my cheeks in, and suppressed a spasm in my throat, squinting hard through involuntary tears.

Manuel pushed his hips against my face, growling loudly, and I shook my head back and forth as I pulled my mouth up his manhood, flicking my tongue. "Ohhh, god, Steve," he hissed, trying to follow my lips. I filled my mouth with his intricately veined girth again, pushing its head hard against the back of my throat as he moaned and bucked, my hands dragging over his lower back, his hips, his thighs, then finally back to his ass. I ran my index finger down the parting of his cheeks and searched for his tight little hole; upon finding it, I pushed on it with the pad of my finger. Manuel released a long sigh, his breath coming loud and fast.

I'd found my rhythm and was bobbing my head up and down his length, stopping at both root and tip, my mouth filling with saliva and precome. I rubbed his asshole with a determined finger, my arm wrapped around his back as my lips went numb. My finger pushed a little harder and Manuel shrieked, then whined an urgent string of, "Please, please, yes, Steven, please!" Acting fast, I dipped my finger in my mouth before I reached between his legs and pushed it into his soft, blossomed rosebud. He released a long cry of surrender, his cock throbbing in my mouth, and I sucked him hard and fast, my finger just barely inside him and pulling forward.

He was thrashing, moaning, gasping over and over, and when I knew he was unbearably close, I let him thrust hard into my mouth, then pushed him as deep in my throat as I could stand. In my mind, I could see the way his arms tensed and his teeth clenched, the veins bulging in his neck, glistening with a layer of sweat. Around my finger and between my lips and in my mouth and throat, I felt the quick spasms of his climax, the hot stream of come threatening to break my composure as it flooded my mouth. With a few final, gentle strokes, I finished him and licked him clean, my lips bright red and my whole mouth tingling. Gripping his hips, I kissed his stomach as he caught his breath, then stood up and untied him. Once freed, Manuel shot his arms out and wrestled me to the floor, onto my back, and kissed me feverishly, laughing and breathing heavily, just as sweet and relaxed as I wanted.

Grinning, I hugged him tightly and mussed his hair. "Feel better?" I asked.

"Mmm-hmm," he hummed into my ear, taking the lobe between his teeth. I thought I'd heard car doors slamming, and suddenly the doorbell rang. Manuel looked up and blushed. "Oh shit..."

I kissed him once more and pushed him up off of me. He sat back against the closet door with his face in his hands, trying to quell his postcoital high. I went to greet our guests at half-mast, a little dizzy and disappointed at this interruption. Soon, Manuel came out of the bedroom, barely containing his endorphin high. "Ah, there you are!" I announced, wrapping my arm around his shoulders and kissing his head. He glowed and smiled and leaned on me as he said his hellos, betraying no hint of his earlier panic.

MAGIC WORDS

Emily Bingham

When I hear the front door being pulled shut and locked, then the noise of a car pulling away, I know it's time.

In preparation for this moment I've dressed in a white sweater, a plaid skirt that barely covers my behind, and matching argyle kneesocks. After dressing up, I have nothing to do in this empty room except wait.

It's hard to tell how long I've been waiting. Every noise puts me on edge with the hope that it will be the signal that I can leave this room. My heart races each time the house settles or a car door slams on the street outside the window. I've been thinking of the sound for so long that it seems like a figment of my imagination at first.

As I finally lift myself from the chair, the air of the room passes over my bare upper legs, bringing my attention to the wetness between them. I run one finger along my labia, shocked at how excited I am. I blush as I realize that daydreaming about the events I've agreed to has made such an impression.

This provides the motivation I need to pull open the door and slowly make my way down the hall; the door at the end of it both beckons and threatens. The anticipation was torture but now that it's over I'm nervous to find out what happens next. I close my eyes while resting my hand on the doorknob, taking in my last moment of solitude.

Once I swing the door open to expose the room on the other side, my stomach drops. Aside from walls lined with books, the floor-to-ceiling window near the desk and the large leather chair at the center of this office, the room is empty.

I feel a bit heartbroken. All that waiting for nothing? It isn't until I turn to leave the room that I hear the floor creak and notice the top of his head resting against the back of the chair. He's so still I overlooked him.

"Leave the door open and come sit in my lap." His voice is deep and calm. It passes through me, causing a chill as I acknowledge I'm willing do every little thing he asks. When he speaks I feel half-hypnotized, unable to deny him. The wetness between my legs increases as I walk toward him.

It isn't fear that makes me slow to cross the room. My concern is the things I am likely to ask him for, the way I asked for this afternoon's game. He has a way about him that makes it safe to say or do the filthiest things. He makes me want to let every deviant thought jump from my lips and into his ear with the hope he will help make it come true.

I feel like the shy schoolgirl I'm dressed as while coming around the front of the chair where he can see me. I sense him shift his weight to sit upright but I can't bring myself to look up and meet his eyes. He makes a small satisfied noise so he must like what he sees, making me feel much less ridiculous in this girlish outfit.

"Be a good girl and come here." He puts his hand out to

guide me. I put my hand in his and allow him to pull me into his lap where it's warm and safe. He wraps me in his arms until my nervous shivering subsides. "Shh, that's my good girl." His strong hands pet my head and pull my face to his chest. We stay together, looking out the window at the clouds passing by.

Eventually he cups my chin in his hand and pulls my head to face him. Not looking at him directly, I still know he's smiling as he passes his fingers softly over my face. When he kisses my forehead I think I'll go crazy with the inability to tilt my face up to meet his lips. I need him so badly—his hands and lips all over me, to feel every inch of him under my fingers. But that isn't part of the game; I can't have these things without him giving them to me first.

I continue waiting for his instructions while my pussy thrums with excitement, smelling the musk coming from between my thighs and realizing he can too. Knowing how much I want him will likely cause him to force me to wait that much longer for what I really want. His gentle form of sadism is to deny the greedy thing inside of me until it suits him to satisfy it.

"Look at me." I raise my face just enough to see his kind eyes hidden behind his glasses. After all this time he can still make me hot with just a look. "You know I love you very much, don't you?" I nod and feel a warm flush course through me.

In this skirt, in his lap, with his hands on me while he's speaking in that fatherly voice, I feel so very small; this in turn makes me excited in a way I'm not accustomed to. He cups my chin between his thumb and forefingers, guiding my face up to make eye contact with him, his serious look making me realize my mistake. He wants me to use my words, which are difficult to eke out around him sometimes. I manage a shaky, "Yes."

The playful edge to his expression lingers a moment before

it's gone, his eyebrow now raised to show he means business. I know what he wants to hear, the word I've agreed to end all of my sentences with and yet can't bear to force from my lips. Just thinking this word makes me queasy.

Looking into his dark eyes, my desire to please him overrules any discomfort about the dreaded word. I start again, hoping the affirmation will be a palate cleanser for the filth that will come after it. "Yes...Daddy."

The shame is a scalding tickle that takes over every cell in my body. Looking down at his lap to hide from his gaze, I feel more embarrassed than in any naked-in-front-of-a-crowd nightmare. It's the one word I promised myself I would never say, yet he has managed to make even this taboo titillating, something I want to explore with him. I'm annoyed at myself for being so aroused by this lone, little word.

He kisses my forehead again, saying, "Good. Now stand up."

As he looks me over, I return the favor, biting my lower lip to hold back a smile as I notice his shiny black shoes, the ones that do unexplainable things to me whenever I see them. Whether on his feet or in his closet, they make me wet. The old-fashioned, gentlemanly quality of them reminds me of every authority figure I've ever had a crush on but could never have.

There's a quiet power that seems to radiate off a man in a suit and tie, both of which he also happens to be wearing. The dark pants hug his curves, hinting at everything I already know is underneath. His white shirt, crisp to the touch when it had been pressed against my face, gives off the scent of his skin and aftershave, that familiar smell that gets caught on my clothing so that I catch subtle hints of him when we're apart. His suit jacket, still warm from his body heat, is casually tossed over the arm of the chair. I like to unbutton and sneak my arms under this jacket while he's still wearing it, feeling the unyielding woolen fabric and the comfort of his heft all at once.

He slides to the front edge of the chair, slipping his knees between my thighs, hands slowly traveling down my sides. His fingers stop just before reaching my hips, using them to pull me closer. In this way he insists, without speaking, that I straddle him. I do so gladly, thrilled to have him close. It's a struggle to keep myself from leaning closer to kiss him with his face almost, but not quite, touching mine.

I reach out to hold him around the waist, steadying myself and enjoying the heat through the fabric of his pants. It takes all of my self-control not to rub myself against him as I settle into a comfortable position. Even kneeling so I rest inches above his crotch, I can feel him stiffen a bit between my legs. I allow a small moan to escape my throat at the cruelty of not being able to touch him there. This makes him snicker knowingly and grab my ass through the skirt, kneading me with his powerful fingers. I paw at his lower back, trying so hard to behave myself.

"My sweet girl," he whispers. I feel one of his hands trace its way up my back until reaching my hair, wrapping around the braids and pulling my head back sharply. I gasp at the suddenness of being drawn away from him and grab the front of his shirt so as not to fall over.

He kisses down my face and throat, tormenting me with his nearness. Using my hair as a handle, he tugs me around, yanking my head back when I attempt to move my mouth to meet his. I am moaning and pleading wordlessly, my breathing gone funny with lust.

When I can't take the denial another second, I whisper, "Please?"

He stops and cocks his head so that his ear is close to my lips. "Please, what?"

"Please, Daddy," I try. He tsks his tongue and pulls my head farther away from him, waiting for me to say the magic words. "Please, Daddy, may I have a kiss?"

"Such a good girl to ask for what you want." The handle of my hair brings me closer this time, so our lips are almost touching, yet he holds me out of reach. My hands claw at his shirt, fingering his buttons and tie, trying to resist the urge to pull him to me. Just when I think I will go mad from frustration, he pulls me forward, kissing me deeply, all soft lips and the perfect amount of tongue dancing against mine. I am panting in his mouth, a starving person finally getting a morsel of something delicious. My hands run through his hair and to the back of his head, hoping to convince him not to stop.

The bulge in his pants grows, making it difficult not to lower myself until my bare cunt rests against the fabric covering his crotch. Instead, I distract myself with the wet throb of his tongue on mine. As I'm relaxing into the lusciousness of his mouth, he pulls me by my hair out of range again.

"Poor thing," he teases in response to the pained noises I make at being denied again. "Stand for me." I look at him in disbelief, unsure that I can trust my lust-weak legs to maneuver out of his lap. "Now!" He doesn't raise his voice; the firmness of his tone is enough.

I stand and look at him pathetically as he motions with his finger that I should turn around. Behind me the chair shifts under his movements but I hear nothing else to hint at what he's up to. Time does the funny thing where it slows to nothing so that it feels like an eternity before I hear the unmistakable noise of his zipper. Then silence.

My heart is frenzied and I can barely contain the urge to turn to him. His cock is almost certainly free of his pants now, just inches away. The idea that I can't see, let alone touch it, is maddening. I want to know what he's doing behind me; I'm on edge waiting for his next instruction.

I'm so focused on waiting that his sudden touch startles me. He chuckles while working his hands under my skirt. Sometimes his hands travel as far as the tops of my thighs in their ministrations but never stray between them. When my behind is so sensitive from his touch that I giggle, he stops.

His hands then work their way down the backs of my thighs, stopping at my knees to push them apart, a hint that I spread them wider. I do, continuing to widen my stance until my legs are as far apart as I can manage comfortably. From the sounds of creaking leather I guess he is leaning back in the chair.

"How about I read you a story?"

Though hearing him narrate a tale to me in his deep voice is one of my favorite activities, it is distinctly not what I was hoping for in this moment. Being a good girl, however, I stand still and say, "Yes, Daddy."

There is more shifting behind me and what sounds like a book being opened, the pages settling in his hands. His voice is low and controlled, a late-night radio deejay purring into the airwaves. "*Lolita, light of my life, fire of my loins. My sin, my soul, Lolita...*" I can't help but giggle at his choice of reading material, nor can I resist being swept away while listening to him read.

He stops and I hear the book being closed, followed by the further unlatching of his pants and belt. "Come sit on Daddy's lap."

He reaches his arm out to guide me as I turn, eagerly moving to sit facing him. He shakes his head, giving me the "turn around" gesture again. Not wanting to displease him, I turn and wait, a bit disappointed I wasn't even given an opportunity to see that part of him I've been longing for all afternoon.

"Sit," he says, using my hips to guide me backward. Convinced this will lead to more chaste reading of Nabokov, I'm surprised when he stops me just above his lap. I feel him adjusting himself. "Sit in my lap properly."

I'm not sure what he means until I realize he's using one hand to guide me lower while the other holds his cock steady, pointing in the direction of my pussy as an offering. The moment his cock touches my lips I realize how warm and inviting he feels. I can't contain myself another second as I slide down the length of him in a rush. Once fully inside me, he grasps my hips, keeping me from moving. "There, that's better."

He wraps his arms around me, holding me close, and kisses my neck. His cock is so hard it's almost painful; this only makes me crave him more. Small noises fall from my lips—moans, cooing and wordless begging—so desperate for him that I'm not even sure what I'm pleading for.

"Shhh," he whispers in my ear. "Shh, darling, it's okay." He continues to hold me still; the lack of moving while so absolutely full of him is torture. I so badly want him to fuck me that I'm unsure how long I can endure this.

He reaches for the book, using his strength to hold my back against his chest with his other hand so I can't move. He reads, this time quieter and closer to my ear, like a bedtime story. "*There might have been no Lolita at all had I not loved, one summer, a certain initial girl-child…*"

He holds me tight to his body as he reads, only letting go for one brief moment to adjust my skirt so that it covers my lap. He drapes it modestly over my thighs so it would appear to anyone watching as if I'm merely sharing the chair with him.

I give in to the situation, enjoying the wickedness of his cock being inside me while I'm hearing a story. It seems dirtier somehow than so many things we've done together. I rest my head against his shoulder, signaling that I'll behave. This allows him to release his grasp and instead pet my hair between turning pages. I reward his trust by only moving ever so slightly to keep him hard and myself interested. Just as I'm settling into the rhythm of his words and becoming engrossed by the story, the front door opens.

My blood goes cold with panic. My first instinct is to bolt out of his lap to keep from getting caught at our game. Instead he holds me still. "It's alright, shh, just stay here and listen to the story."

Though I trust him completely, this is the hardest thing he's ever asked of me. How can he be so calm? The door is wide open; anyone could walk into this room. He continues reading but I have lost track of the story. I'm focused on the sound of someone entering the house and sense the horrible eventuality of them heading in our direction.

Before there's time to think about disentangling myself from his lap, footsteps travel quickly down the hall and stop at the door frame. The reading stops. I'm too terrified to look up and find out who's standing there.

He turns his head to greet the visitor, resting the book on my legs, with his arms around me. "Hi, we're just doing some reading." I feel his cock jump to attention, the adrenaline of being caught seeming to add to the excitement.

"That's sweet." There is no edge of concern to the female voice, as if she hasn't a clue the depravity occurring in front of her. She walks toward us and the urge to flee occurs to me again. Surely if she gets any closer it will become obvious that we're mid-fuck. He subtly squeezes me, reminding me to keep still.

Recounting the events of her day in great detail, it's obvious that she's too absorbed in herself to notice anything else, or maybe she doesn't care. Finally I look up and see that this is of course the friend who's staying in the guest room this week. Who else would have a key to the door? I feel silly for having been so worried.

She crosses the room to stand over the chair, as if she wants to be invited to join us. When neither of us moves to encourage her diatribe on the lack of quality organic groceries, she smiles and leaves, saying, "Well then, I'm going to make some dinner, I'll let you know when it's ready."

She has no clue. I can't help but grin at how much we've just gotten away with.

He pulls my face around to him and I see he's smiling as well. We kiss, me contorting to meet his lips, his cock still inside me. Distracted by fondling my chest, he loses his grip on the book; the sound of it hitting the ground startles us both. We laugh for a moment before catching ourselves, looking in the direction of the kitchen, stifling our laughter by kissing deeply.

At any moment, I expect him to tell me to be a good girl and stand up so we can get on with the evening, not wanting to chance getting caught again. Instead he puts a hand at the back of my head so I can't pull away from his lips. He increases the force of his kiss, making me so enthralled by his mouth that it takes me a second to notice he has started to move his hips. Once I realize that what I've wanted all afternoon is finally happening, I rock my body in time with his. When he doesn't stop me, I use what leverage I can get with stocking feet on the slippery floor to move up and down in his lap, bouncing on his cock with enthusiasm.

The door to the room is still open so that we can clearly hear the noises of pots and pans from a room away. It would take very little to catch her attention, causing her to come back into the room out of curiosity. Given our flushed state and the smell of sex permeating the room, there's no way to play innocent any longer; even she would notice what we were up to.

He feels so good sliding easily in and out of my pussy that it isn't long before I mutter into his mouth breathlessly, "I'm going to come."

"Mmm. You're going to come for Daddy?" he whispers in the nape of my neck.

"Yes, Daddy." I hold on to the moment, feeling ready to peak, desperate to relieve this full-body ache. Every muscle tightens until I can't wait another second but know better than to come without his permission.

"Be a good girl and come for me."

Those words are all the encouragement I need, so when he also snakes a finger between my legs to gently rub my clit, I'm a total goner. I come so hard I put my own fingers in my mouth to keep from crying out. My pussy clenches around him while he rides the wave of my climax, bucking against me, still fingering my clit.

Just as my body hints at a second orgasm, he startles me to attention by pulling me against him so sharply that my feet lift off the floor. He thrusts in and out of me in a frenzy. I feel him come inside me, mingling with my puddle of excitement to make a sticky mess.

"Such...a...good...girl," he barely manages between breaths. I come again, listening to the squish of our bodies meeting. When his satiated cock slips out in the midst of my orgasm, so does a warm dribble of our combined juices, the pearly trails moistening the front of his pants and my inner thighs. I run my fingers through it, enjoying the mess we've created.

The delighted noise he makes while watching forces me out of my reverie. I half expect to be in trouble for ruining his nice clothes until he says with a smirk, "Look what you did." We laugh naughtily at each other for a moment until I turn to kiss him deeply, finally able to wrap my arms around him, feeling his heart race through his shirt and tie.

"Now go get cleaned up and help in the kitchen." He smiles and smacks my butt gently. Satisfied and grinning, I leave to set the table.

POLKA-DOT DRESS

Erzabet Bishop

T hat dress is going to give one of your fellow contestants heat stroke," Sorcha commented as she guided the zipper up Justine's back. "You're really going through with it?" She reached the top and then stepped toward the bed, her face pensive. Sorcha threw her own hair up in a clip, letting the errant curls fall down the back of her head. Tonight she sported her green O'Malley's T-shirt and her skinniest jeans.

Justine grinned. "I know. Me in a pinup-style dress. Who'd have thought?" She touched up the black eyeliner framing her dark-brown eyes and let her lips curve up in a cat-that-got-the-cream smile. For a moment she almost missed her usual black leathers but getting a load of herself in the mirror was worth it. "This is a onetime shot. And only because Ameliah dared me."

"I just can't believe I have to work tonight of all nights. If Brea calls out one more time I'm going to take her out back and give her a piece of my mind. I'm tired of covering for her every time she gets a pinky-toe ache." Sorcha pouted and reached for her shoes. "Now I'm missing your girly girl debut on Vintage Night."

"Bitch."

"I know." Sorcha sighed. "I'm pissed. Last Friday night she called out too. A migraine. *Really?*" She tucked the bar shirt into her jeans and sat on the bed to tie her sneakers. "So...she dared you, huh?"

"What do you think? Falsies or mascara?"

Sorcha stood up and eyed the makeup tray. "Oh god. The last time I wore those damned things one fell in my drink." She shuddered. "Here. Wear this one." Sorcha handed Justine a tube of lash-exploding black mascara. "It'll make your lashes look bigger without having something looking like a fake spider on your face. You didn't answer my question."

Justine aimed the wand at her eye and paused. "If I don't answer, you can deny all knowledge if she asks you when she comes home with me tonight." She applied the mascara. "You didn't glue the falsies down enough. They aren't supposed to fall off like that." She chuckled. "Besides, it's only Pinup Night, not a beauty contest." *And then next week I'll be back in my leathers.*

"And how do you know?" Sorcha narrowed her eyes. "Jeez, woman. I go to clubs in girl wear more than you do." Sorcha's gaze grew pensive. "So, are you going to spill about the sudden change in, um, style? You could put a rockabilly chick in a permanent coma with the way that polka-dot dress is clinging to your boobs. "

"That's the point, chica." Justine winked. She reached for the tray of lipstick Sorcha brought out and paused, undecided. "What color?"

"Oh. Go for this one. The wine red will rock the red in the

dress. And those kick-ass shoes." Sorcha picked out a shiny silver tube. "Here. Try it."

Justine uncapped the tube and set the top on the tray. The lipstick popped up and she slid the sensual red color over her lips in a deliberate swipe. "How's that?" She made a moue with her lips and blinked her eyes.

"Hussy." Sorcha giggled. "Okay. So I won't ask. You look like you should be baking cookies in someone's kitchen."

Justine grinned. "Now there's something. Find Ana and some wooden spoons and that would be the most fun batch of cookies that never got made."

"Very funny. So she likes to spank me. You should talk." Sorcha's eyes twinkled with mischief. So...are you wearing it? Under the dress? You said tonight was the night." Sorcha reached down to flip the corner of the dress up.

"I don't know what you mean." Justine made a show of gathering her compact and the borrowed lipstick and tucking them into her bag.

"You are *such* a liar."

Justine pursed her now-dark red lips. "Don't you need to get to your shift?"

Sorcha twisted her wrist to check out the time. "Shit. Yeah. You're right. If I'm late one more time my boss is going to ream me."

"Mmm-hmm."

"But I'm still not moving until you spill about tonight."

"Go to work, why don't you? If you get fired, who's going to share the rent?"

"Maybe you can ask little miss sexy britches. I'm sure once she gets a load of you in that polka-dot number she'll be swooning at your feet in a puddle of drool."

"Ha ha."

"I'm impressed you got your nails done too. Those red peep shoes are awesome with that polish."

Justine scooped her clutch off the bed, sending her a mutinous glare. "Go. Seriously."

"Yeah, yeah," Sorcha called out. She relocated from the bedroom and Justine heard her fussing in the kitchen. "You better text me later! If Ana comes over after work, we'll be checking out those spoons." She yanked a microwave meal out of the freezer and snagged an apple from the bowl on the counter. "Oh, Justine?"

She paused at the kitchen entryway. "Yeah?"

"You're hot. She's gonna love it."

"I hope so." Justine didn't realize she had been holding her breath until she released it.

"Go. Have fun. Be a grrrl."

"Yes, mom." Justine shook her head and let the corner of her lip quirk up in a begrudging smile. She did look good in the dress. She preferred her leathers to a dress any day of the week, but she still held on to one concession. Justine smiled at the familiar weight of the harness beneath the feminine frippery. Her girl wanted her to play along. Okay. *Fine.* She was going to show her just what she was made of. Even if she broke her ankle on the way down the stairs.

Ameliah had to work the mid shift at her job, so she was meeting Justine at the Sapphire Club. The night couldn't have been set up better if she had worked that out herself. As she made her way up the walk, Justine admired the lush garden and Gothic-style architecture that gave the building its charm. All gray stone and graceful lines, it looked like an English manor house. Justine reached the door and fumbled in the small reticule for her ID. The bouncer, Marco, handed it back to her with a wink.

"You have fun now, Justine. Don't break too many hearts in that getup."

Justine threw back her head and laughed. "See you later." She waded into the crowded entrance to the club and stopped to watch the crowd. Everyone was dressed to the nines. Old-fashioned movie stars in tuxedos flirted with blonde starlets dripping in sparkling dresses reminiscent of the Gatsby era. Barely clothed pinup girls posed on stage for the weekly competition. The tinkling of glass and smell of women's perfume filled the air. It was refreshing to be back. She should try out but there was only one thing on her mind. She needed to find Ameliah.

The sea of partiers parted and there she was. Ameliah's barely there dress cascaded down her body like a sheer negligee out of an erotic ghost story. Her nipples winked through the gauzy fabric and as she moved Justine got a hint of the dark thatch of hair at the apex of her thighs. A mixture of lust and anger that she would wear that dress in public raced through her veins. She covered the distance in seconds flat, standing in front of her lover.

"Justine! You made it." Ameliah's long brown hair was spun into a confection of curls parted on the side, framing her face. Her lips were painted a dark reddish brown, making her hazel eyes pop.

"So did you, I see." Her tone was dangerous and Ameliah took a step back, her eyes widening.

"What's wrong?"

"Come with me." Justine grabbed her hand and stalked to the back of the club. She shoved open the lounge door and yanked Ameliah inside. The lounge was filled with couches and a television, an area where members could come and rest before they continued with their night. One wall held mirrors and a counter for makeup application. The other led into the restroom. Justine clicked the latch on the door and turned to face Ameliah.

"I go to the trouble to wear peep shoes and a dress and you show up in a see-through night gown. What are you thinking woman?"

Ameliah's lips curved up into a grin. "So you noticed."

"Of course I did. I'm not blind." Justine's tone was incredulous. She pulled Ameliah into her arms, her breasts sliding against the slippery fabric of the dress. "I might combust though. Damn, woman. You're going to kill me yet. Every woman out there is thinking about nibbling on those thighs."

"I've been waiting for you," Ameliah whispered, her voice husky. "Nibble away. You wore a dress. I like it. You should enter the competition."

"Sorry, other plans." Justine's lips met hers in a heated kiss. Her hands slid down Ameliah's backside, cupping her ass and dragging her forward. "That's not all."

Ameliah gasped. "You wore it. Under the dress?"

"I did." Justine gave her a cocky grin.

"Oh! Let me see!" Ameliah reached out to touch the hem.

Justine slapped her hand away. "Nope. My turn. Bend over the counter. I want to see your face in the mirror when you come."

"Oh really?"

"Yes." Justine moved behind Ameliah, her hands reaching around her body to pull her against her breasts. She ground her mound into her ass and cupped her breasts, massaging them, letting her feel what she would be missing if she didn't obey.

"Last instruction. Then I walk." Justine let go and stepped back, her body churning with desire. Her own nipples were hard, her clit throbbing between her legs.

"Yes, Ma'am." Ameliah gave her a saucy glare and assumed

the position. She eased herself forward, parting her legs so she was leaning on the makeup counter. The sheer dress draped down, giving Justine a hazy view of what she had been lusting after.

Justine reached beneath the sheer fabric and let her fingers wander into the slick folds between Ameliah's legs. Her thighs were coated with juices. Justine slid her finger inside of Ameliah's hot, soaked channel.

"Oh goddess. Take me!" Ameliah squirmed, straining against her hand.

"Always in such a hurry." Justine flicked a thumb across her clit and Ameliah stifled a groan.

A harsh curse and a sudden banging started on the door to the lounge. "Hey! You're not supposed to lock the door."

"Are you ready, babe? Looks like they didn't give us much time tonight."

"Fuck me. Please!"

Justine flipped up the flouncy red dress and secured the strap on the harness. She pulled the long curved dildo the color of her skin into position and moved behind her lover.

Ameliah's eyes followed her in the mirror, her lips parting in desire.

"Have you been thinking about me today while you were at work?" Justine ran her fingers down Ameliah's back, sliding the fabric up. She leaned forward and slid the tip of the dildo against the tight opening of Ameliah's sex. She teased her by sliding in just a fraction before pulling out.

Ameliah angled back for more, a cry escaping her lips.

"So greedy. And here I was ready to take my time, give you the fucking you so richly deserve. Should I give it to you now or make you wait?"

The banging on the door started again in earnest.

Ameliah opened her legs wider and angled her ass higher, giving Justine greater access. "No! Please, Justine. Don't leave me like this!"

"They'll be here any minute," Justine taunted. She placed a tender kiss on her lover's neck, leaving a lipstick mark on the pale flesh.

"Fuck. Me."

"Such a dirty mouth on such a lovely girl," Justine whispered, rimming Ameliah's sex with her cock. "I may have a use for it when I get you home."

Justine slid deep inside, pressing her cock into Ameliah's tight pussy. She began to thrust, reaching around to fondle Ameliah's breasts. The image they made in the mirror was startling. Ameliah's fever-bright eyes watched her every move. It excited her all the more knowing Ameliah could see every expression on her face as she took her, with everyone on the other side of the door aware of just what was going on.

"Do you want to come?" Justine purred.

"Yes!"

"Ask me nicely." Justine thrust again, holding her body against Ameliah's hard enough that her own pussy spasmed from the pressure of the dildo on her clit. They were both so close.

Justine began to glide inside of her channel, letting the pressure build inside of her. "Come now!" Justine slammed into her pussy, filling Ameliah as deep as she could go. Her fingers fumbled, searching for Ameliah's clit. She stroked and fondled the erect nub.

"Come now!" Justine moaned, setting her hips in a grinding motion so she could bury her cock as deep as she could go.

Ameliah cried out, her body shuddering in Justine's arms as she herself was flung far into the electrical charges of liquid ecstasy. She breathed in deep, soul-drenching drafts of air and shattered into a million glowing stars.

A key in the lock brought them both back to reality. "Hurry. Your dress." Justine slid out and slipped Ameliah's dress back down over her hips. She unhitched the harness strap, letting the dildo fall against her thigh. She flipped her dress down just as the door opened, the angry manager storming thorough the room.

"What are you two doing in here?" Her eyes narrowed on the two women suspiciously.

Ameliah smiled. "Justine was just helping me in a moment of distress. Sorry!" She tugged Justine's hand, leading her out of the lounge, through the club and out into the night.

"And where do you think you're taking me?"

"Back to your place, of course. That dress needs a wooden spoon and a smile and I know just how to give it to you."

"Scandalous." Justine kissed her, watching the way the diaphanous fabric draped across her lover's ass as she broke free and darted ahead toward the car. *Mine.*

BABY STEPS

Justine Elyot

It slipped through my fingers like lost dreams, pleasures I had forgotten. Silk, lace; even glossy, watery latex, giving my skin the sensual attention it had craved for too long.

The door banged downstairs and I slammed the suitcase lid and shoved it under the bed.

"Are you about, love?"

I picked up the baby and made my way to the top of the stairs, looking down at Ryan's back as he took off his coat and scarf and hung them on the peg. Neat, tidy, ready for a kit inspection at all times. I guessed that was what ten years of navy training did for a man.

"Good day?"

He turned and smiled.

"Ach, you know. Something smells gorgeous."

It wasn't me he was talking about, not these days. I'd gone from citrus scents by big fashion houses to milky spit-up without passing Go.

"It's a while since I made a steak and ale pie," I said. "Thought you might be feeling deprived."

Ryan bent to kiss Will's head, then my cheek.

Will reached out and pulled his dad's tie so hard he started coughing.

I prised off the tiny fingers and laughed.

"I'll see if I can put him down. Keep an eye on the pie for me, will you? Don't want a burnt crust."

I'd been assiduous about wearing Will out with fresh air and nonstop play today and thank goodness my tactics paid off. He drifted into the land of Nod while the mobile was still pinging out "Hickory Dickory Dock."

I don't know why I was feeling so anxious. It was as if the zoo animals on the mobile were rotating inside me, the little tune twanging at my nerves.

I didn't have to say anything. I could just leave it. The sex wasn't so bad, anyway. It was just...quotidian. It reminded me of the phrase "on duty" and Ryan working nights at the dockyard. But quotidian wasn't the same as rubbish, and the last thing I wanted to do was hurt him or make him feel inadequate.

I could just leave it. Eat the pie, eat the ice cream, drink a glass of wine, cuddle in front of the TV and then maybe...

No. I was going to go ahead with the plan. If it worked, I could get my red-hot sexy minx self back without saying anything about finding the post-baby sex boring. If it worked.

The steak pie was perfect and the bottle of red complemented it perfectly. Everything was perfect. Perfect husband, perfect baby, perfect house.

"I've been thinking," I blurted after a blow-by-blow account of Will's day.

Ryan looked wary. Perhaps those were the wrong words to choose.

"Don't look so scared." I laughed nervously. "It has been known to happen."

"I've been thinking too," he said, leaning forward. He smiled at me, but the smile was weirdly sympathetic. "We need a holiday."

"Oh," I said, temporarily derailed. "That would be lovely, but that wasn't what I was thinking."

"No? Okay, what then?"

I took a gulp of wine then a deep breath.

"Now Will's a bit older and I've got the remnants of my brain back together, I thought I might get myself a little job."

Ryan frowned. "You said you didn't want to put him in nursery. The money's okay, Jess, we've got it covered."

"No, I wouldn't need childcare. It's something I could do from home. Flexible hours, whenever I like."

"Not thinking of going on the game, are you?" he said, but I could tell he wasn't quite joking.

"It would give me an interest in life outside toddler groups and Barney the bloody Dinosaur. God, I hate that purple bastard."

Ryan sniggered and started singing the "I Love You" song.

"Shut up!" I made a threatening gesture with my fork.

"Ooh, someone's feeling brave," he said, with a look in his eye that made my stomach flip. It had been so long since I'd seen it, so long, and I used to live for it.

It made me smile and put down my fork.

"Yeah," I said softly. "So what you gonna do about it, sailor boy?"

"Don't rush me," he said. "I'm thinking about it."

"Really?"

The silence stretched into unease.

"If...I mean...would you be okay?" he said.

"Ryan, I'm not made of glass."

"It's just, y'know, you're the mother of my son now."

"You see me differently." I sounded sad. I felt sad. "But I'm the same person."

"I know you are. I know." But he was trying to convince himself.

He needed a more practical form of persuasion. I pressed on.

"Ryan, this job I'm thinking of."

"Oh, yeah. That. Go on."

"It's hosting parties in people's homes. An evening or two a week."

"You're going to be an Avon lady? Ding dong."

"That kind of thing but...different."

I bit my lip and looked up at him from under lowered eyelashes, the way I used to in the pre-baby days when a spanking was on the cards.

He took in a sharp breath.

"Naughty knickers?"

I nodded.

"Jess! Seriously? You want to do that?"

"I want to do it, Ryan. I get my adult social life back, I get to be a taxpaying member of society again, I make a bit of pin money and a lot of commission."

"Commission?" He liked the idea. His eyes had gone from hooded to wide and bright. "As in..."

"Anything I like from the catalogue."

"And, er, would you happen to have a copy of that catalogue lying around, by any chance?"

"Oh, I can do better than that, sailor boy. Come upstairs and I'll show you. Actually—no! Don't. Wait there and I'll come to you."

I pushed back my chair and ran, giggling, to the stairs.

My heart was beating ten to the dozen, just the way it used to when I saw him turn the corner of my street, full of swagger and wicked intentions for me.

I pulled out the suitcase and sorted through it with trembling hands, trying to decide whether to go for the red satin corset and thong or the bottomless PVC dress.

Oh god, I was so tempted by the PVC, but was it too much too soon? The red corset would be playing it safe. It was sexy but vanilla—"come hither" but not "spank me."

I wanted a spanking, though.

I put the corset back.

This PVC dress would be a severe test of my post-baby body. I was pretty sure it was back to normal, but did the mirror lie? The PVC would not.

I took off my jeans and sweater, then the big knickers and maternity bra I still wore as a kind of safety net, despite the fact I was no longer breastfeeding. I had been loath to get rid of them, perhaps unready to move on from Will's tiny baby days. He was growing up too quickly and I didn't want to acknowledge it.

But it was definitely time to dump the frumpy bra. I threw it into the bedroom bin, blinking hard to make the wrench more bearable, then I went to the full-length mirror and took a long, hard look.

Stretch marks, but they weren't a problem—Ryan loved them. Wish I could have kept my stunning panto-dairymaid tits, but nature wouldn't oblige—all the same, they were good, high and firm and rosy-nippled. My pubic hair was neatly trimmed, something I'd come to enjoy doing after months of not being able to see below my stomach. My waist was smaller than my hips again, thank god, and my legs had never really changed. I could do this. I could carry off this naughty PVC number, just as I'd swanned around the house in corsets and thigh-highs not so long ago.

It was a bit of a struggle to get the thing on, but I'd been expecting that. It was a basic sleeveless shift design, cut low at the bust and tight around the ribs so my breasts were lifted high, two bouncy balls in close captivity. The most radical design feature was the complete lack of bottom coverage—there was a shiny black strip of material above and another below, at thigh level, but in between my perky cheeks peeked out, begging for attention.

I looked in the mirror again, front and back, and felt myself get wet without even touching. The dress felt so snug, so cold, so cruelly tight, and I was so exposed. I was on display, and I might as well have been wearing a big placard around my neck saying SPANK ME.

Well, just in case that message wasn't perfectly clear...

I went back to the suitcase and bent—not without some loss of breath—over it. If my bottom had been covered, I was pretty sure a seam would have split. That was how tight it was. I was feeling a bit hot already, but that just added to the gathering tension between my legs.

Underneath the lube gift-packs and massage-oil burners, way beneath the leopard-print bodysuit and the ribbon-bondage ties, was the thing I sought. I laid my fingers on the handle and pulled it out. It was a ruler paddle, in bright red flexible plastic with cutout letters forming the word SLUT. At the end, as if in apology, was a cutout heart shape.

Here I was, then, ready for my spanking.

I just hoped Ryan was too.

"Are you okay up there?" he called.

"Ssh," I hissed from the top of the stairs. "You'll wake Will."

I had on a pair of heels I hadn't worn in eighteen months and

I had to take the stairs carefully, holding on to the banister. So much for a grand entrance—but at least Ryan was in the dining area and couldn't see me.

His eyes nearly fell out of his head when I did my best heel-to-toe Marilyn wiggle into the room.

"Fuck," he said.

"Good idea."

"Whoa."

Reduced to inarticulacy—always a good sign.

Spurred on by this initial success, I went to kneel in front of him.

He looked down at my breasts, his Adam's apple bobbing. He hadn't even seen the back of the dress yet.

"What've you got there?" he said, pointing at the paddle.

I held it up for him.

"I've been a bad girl, Sir," I said.

He took it from me. I didn't know what he thought. He was breathing fast, looking a little tormented.

"Can we?" he said, looking over at the baby monitor.

"Turn it off," I suggested. "If he starts bawling we'll hear him."

"Yeah, but will *he* hear *us*?"

"He's asleep, Ryan. He's upstairs, through two shut doors. And we'll keep it down."

"Really? You've changed, then."

"Gag me," I said urgently. "Get a drying-up cloth and gag me."

He sprang up, almost knocking me back on my heels, and took a cloth from the drawer. He took the opportunity to knock the monitor off the counter and into that same drawer, closing it with a flourish.

"Okay," he said. "You've got it. And you're going to get it.

I want to see you on your feet, hands flat on the chair, bum in the air, girl."

I was only too happy to obey, trying to stifle giggles. I was a terrible giggler and had been spanked for it more times than I could remember.

He came behind me with the cloth, but instead of bending to tie it around my head, he stopped dead and said, "Jesus Christ, Jess. You really *need* this, don't you?"

"It's been so long," I whispered.

His hand landed on my bare cheeks, caressing them slowly until my clit was itching and soaked.

"You need it," he repeated, hooking a finger into the buckled strap that crossed my thighs and pulling at it. "So, so badly."

"Yes."

"Say it."

"I need a spanking, really, really badly."

He paused, prior to gagging me.

"You're sure?" he said.

"It'll be fine," I said. He was the one in need of reassurance, not me. "Lots of kids have kinky parents. It doesn't mean they have to know about it. Will sleeps like a top these days; those broken nights seem to be over, thank god."

"I'm going to build a shed," said Ryan, and it seemed like such a non sequitur that I burst out laughing, but after a moment, I caught on.

"A woodshed?"

"Exactly. Then we can leave him asleep with the patio doors open and the monitor on, creep down the garden and..."

"Splinters," I said, grimacing.

He laughed.

"I wouldn't worry about splinters, love. Not with what you've got coming to you."

The tea towel was folded and pressed to my mouth, then tied behind. We'd never invested in a proper gag, because Ryan loved to hear my cries and sometimes carry on cruel little conversations in the process of thrashing me. Gags just weren't our kind of fun.

But tonight it was probably for the best.

"You won't be able to safeword," he realized, finishing his knot. "So we'd better have a safe gesture. Kick off your shoes if you want to stop, yeah?"

I nodded. Actually, I wouldn't mind kicking them off right now. My ankles were starting to complain at their unaccustomed usage.

"Okay," whispered Ryan, and I could feel him bending over me, feel his shadow and sense what he held in his hand. There was a long, long pause, then he said, "Shit. I don't know if I can."

I wiggled my bottom desperately, growling through the folded linen map of some Greek island we'd visited on holiday.

Oh! The stroke rung out, a fat, obscene slapping sound that seemed to carry along the street. How it stung! I'd completely forgotten that spankings actually hurt.

"That was too hard, wasn't it?" said Ryan, sounding agitated. "I've gone in too hard. I should have warmed up."

I shook my head and stuck out my bum for more, despite the bar of pain and the heat that radiated from it. I didn't care if it hurt—it was meant to hurt. What I cared about was my husband getting his dominant confidence back and ripping off the "fragile" sticker he'd apparently mentally stamped all over me.

"You're sure?"

"Nurghr!"

He caught a breath. "Right. Right. I'm on it. I'm…"

The paddle fell again, not quite as hard, but beautifully parallel to the first stroke, just below.

"*On it!*" he said triumphantly.

I purred, low down in my throat. This was the touch I remembered.

The strokes came in blissful succession, just hard enough to set that sweet burn into motion but not so hard that I'd bruise. I remembered the word on the paddle and longed to see it, especially when he started covering his previous strokes.

Not only was that painful, it made me worry he'd blur the lettering. I did so want to read the writing on the rear. Mind you, it would be backward, since I'd have to do it in the mirror. Unless he took a photo.

My train of thought stuttered, interrupted as it frequently was by another flash of plastic pain.

In between strokes, I pictured my bottom, framed by the tight, shiny dress, bright red and adorned with the word SLUT in a cascade from the crest of my buttocks to the buckle strap across my thighs.

My groaning was more lust than pain by the time he put the paddle aside and untied my gag.

"You should see yourself," he said, freeing my mouth for a rough grabbing and tongue-probing. After a long, hungry kiss, he repeated his words, then added, "You should see your bum."

"Show me then. Take a picture," I urged.

He went to the coat pegs and got his phone. I felt the flash light everything around me, then smiled and purred when he put the result in front of my face.

My bottom was deep red, except for the crisply outlined white letters. Ryan had laid the strokes perfectly, turning me into a living advertisement for what I was, and what I wanted to be for him tonight.

He had moved well beyond worrying about mishandling me. He unbuckled the strap that held my thighs together and patted them apart, his intention clear.

I chuckled and pushed my bottom out farther, feeling the sticky heat at the tops of my thighs and in the space between. This fuck, this thrusting of him into me, took us back to what we had been, and changed what we had become.

Inside my head, I was in a hundred places, a hundred past memories. I was bent over that pile of tarry rope in the darkened dockyard, my jeans around my knees, looking out all the time for the security patrol. I was tied to a chair with my legs wide, watching Ryan's face as he teased my clit with a vibrator, taking me away from the edge so many times before allowing me to tumble over it. I was lying on my stomach while he poured lube onto my spread bottom cheeks, after a long campaign of persuasion to try anal. I wondered afterward what I'd been so afraid of. I wanted to do it again, wanted to do everything now, wanted Ryan to know that nothing was off limits.

"Do what you want," I panted while he jolted me over and over the bench. "Don't hold back."

He responded by wetting his fingers in my juices and twisting them slowly into my anus while he fucked my pussy even harder. He held them there like an anchor, using his penetration of my tight hole to keep me in position.

I was heading right out of control, a dizzy, delirious mess of sex and need.

"Got what you wanted, didn't you?" he gasped into my ear. "Getting it now."

"Mmm," was all I could say. The old us was leaking into the new us, mixing up the pieces of the jigsaw and rearranging the picture.

I was bent over, spanked, sore, filled in both holes, only

allowed to make a sound because he'd removed the gag, and I
was Me the slut as well as Me the mother. I was those things
and more things and all the things bled together, but right now
I wanted nothing but my orgasm.

I clenched all the muscles I had, tightening my grip on him,
wanting him to feel as big as possible inside me. The friction
burned and pushed me higher. I thrust my hips upward, making
his moves even stronger and deeper.

"Fuck," he said, sounding awestruck. "You gorgeous slut."

Here it was. The blending was complete and the time had
come.

I sucked him in, sucked his orgasm into mine, two separate
climaxes flowing into one, just as our two bodies were joined at
the roots. This was how we had made our baby, but it was also
how we had made us.

I lay slumped over the table for some time, accepting his
kisses on my damp hair and salty skin.

"That was good?" he asked, as if he needed to.

"Exactly what I needed," I said.

"Me too."

After he pulled out, he went to check that the baby monitor
was still working. It was.

"Not a peep out of His Lordship either."

"I told you he was sleeping well these days."

"I'm going to take a shower, then I'm going online to shop
for a woodshed."

"I'll join you."

I took off the latex dress and put the slut paddle back in the
suitcase. I was going to have to buy them now. Looked like my
new career was on.

ON LOCATION

D. L. King

F ondle your balls. Now squeeze them. Grind your ass against that seat, baby. I want to see it in your face. I want to see just exactly what that butt plug is doing to you. You can do better than that. Squeeze harder; show me you mean it. Stroke that hard cock, Harris, and come for me. Yes, baby, come for me, that's right."

I groaned, and three good spurts of semen erupted from the head of my cock. I shuddered, opened my eyes and looked at Dawn's face smiling at me from my laptop screen. I smiled back. Hot come quickly became cold spooge.

"Ooh, Harris, that was fun. I always thought vid cam sex would be crappy or unsexy, but that was fun. Did you think it was fun?"

"Hang on a sec," I said. I turned away from the screen to grab a Kleenex. Mopping myself up, I looked at Dawn. "Yeah, it was fun. We should do it again. Next time I'll make you come."

"Who says I didn't? Hey, you have that thing coming up. What did you decide, train or car?"

Dawn was talking about my film. I was a filmmaker—at least, that was my long-term plan—and I had to do some location scouting for my latest project. I wanted to check out some Bronx locations and maybe even one or two in Staten Island, but the problem was my choices were pretty remote.

I live in Brooklyn and I consider the entire city to be my oyster. I've always known that I could get anywhere I needed to go on the train, so I don't own a car. 'Course, I never needed to go to remote locations in the two boroughs I know nothing about. Well, it seems you can't get *anywhere* on the train, after all. I was going to have to rent a car for this.

"I asked Stan," I said. Stan was a friend of ours who taught at a college in the Bronx. "He was virtually no help at all. As he put it, 'I don't usually cruise vacant lots and marshes.' Hang on a minute."

I stood up, turned around and braced myself against the seat of my desk chair.

"Mmm, very nice," Dawn said.

"Well, if you like that, you'll probably like this even better— or not," I said over my shoulder. I wagged my butt and then reached between my legs, wrapped my fingers around the base of the stainless-steel plug in my ass and slowly pulled. I love the way it feels coming out of me—the pressure, the stretching, the emptiness. And it was fun taunting Dawn, who liked to be the one doing the extracting.

"Hey, who told you to take that out? I might have wanted to come over there and retrieve it myself—you don't know."

"Yeah, well, that's what you get for wanting to have phone sex or computer sex or whatever. And I'm cold." I walked away from the computer. I could vaguely hear her telling me what I could and couldn't do in her presence. I came back wearing a pair of sweats.

"Hey! I don't know if I like this. You think you can do whatever you want because I'm not there."

She was pouting because I'd put on pants without asking permission but that's the thing about using technology for sex. You can do whatever you want. There's nothing the computer can do about it. Maybe she'd make me pay the next time we were together, but for now, I was king of my domain.

"So, this car you're renting, does it have GPS?"

"No, I couldn't afford it. I thought about it but I'll just have to MapQuest stuff really well."

"Well, if I come with you, we can use the GPS on my phone and I can be your navigator."

Dawn and I have been together for five years. I think we'll be together for another fifty. We haven't taken the cohabitation step yet, but I love her dearly and it's not too far off. She's a little crazy and she's more interested in watching films than in making them, but it would be good to have someone along to get lost with, so I said okay. After all, what could happen?

Scenes from *The Bonfire of the Vanities* briefly flashed through my mind.

"Great," she said. "Hey, you know, that really was fun. Later." The image of her clicked off.

It *was* kind of fun. I hadn't thought I'd like it, as I really despise looking at myself on camera, on the computer. But this was different because I wasn't looking at me, I was looking at Dawn, and she looked great. And she must not have thought I looked too stupid because I could see that she had enjoyed watching me, too.

I met Stan for drinks at our favorite downtown bar. Over a couple of vodka cranberries, he explained how to drive to the Bronx, but the words weren't making sense to me. I don't know if it was because I'd only heard about some of these streets on the morning traffic report or because the bartender liked us. And by *liked us*, I mean we were drinking tumblers of slightly pink vodka.

I told him not to worry about it, that I'd find my own way, and we stumbled out to get some dinner.

The following Friday, Dawn showed up at my place with pizza and beer. We spent most of the evening working out how to get from one place to another. She'd pulled out a subway map and put Xs in the general vicinity for each location, and then we'd figured out the most expedient route from place to place. We decided to head to the Bronx first and then, if there was enough time and light, go out to Staten Island.

Neither of us are exactly morning people, so it was a very quick fuck and right to sleep. Even so, I should have known something was up.

The alarm went off at seven, which is criminal on a Saturday, but we rolled out of bed, put on some clothes—sweats and a T-shirt for me, a cotton sundress for her. I made coffee and toasted some bagels for breakfast while Dawn finished getting ready. I grabbed our schedule and the map and Dawn grabbed a beach bag as we headed for the door. "Hey, what's in that?" I asked.

"Just some stuff we might need," she said.

"Like what?"

"Oh, you know, snacks, bottles of water, a notebook, a flashlight. Just stuff. You never know what you might need. It's good to be prepared."

We picked up the car and made it to the first location in about forty-five minutes. There was very little traffic and we only got lost once. We started in the southeastern section, right on the East River. It took a little doing to get down to the water where there were old pilings and tall grasses. Not a soul was

around. Dawn followed me down to the water's edge. I took
a few pictures with my phone and wondered aloud how tall
the weeds were. Dawn rummaged around in her beach bag and
handed me a tape measure.

"Wow, thanks, that's great." I measured the weeds and she
handed me a notebook and pen to jot the measurements down.
"Okay, that's it." I started to head back up the bank.

"Where are you going?" she asked.

"Well, that's it. I got what I needed," I said. "We can go to
the next place."

"Not so fast, buddy. I didn't get what I needed. Bring your
little butt over here."

I carefully made my way back down to the water's edge.
"Take your pants down and bend over," she said.

"What? You can't be serious."

"Come on, there's no one here. No one's gonna see," she
reasoned. "And besides, you still owe me from the other day." I
gave her a questioning look. "On the webcam."

I shook my head but did as she said. I figured she'd spank me
for putting my pants on and we'd be on our way. First, I heard
her rummaging in her bag again and before I knew what was
happening, I felt her lubed-up finger at my asshole. I grabbed my
pants and stood up. "What are you doing?" I asked.

"Just relax, Harris."

"You can't do that here!"

"Sure I can. Why not? Is there a law against it?" she asked.

"Well, as a matter of fact, yes, I think there is a law against
it, and besides, you can't do that here," I repeated, this time
with more conviction.

"There's nobody here to see. But if you waste any more time,
that could change, so I think you'd better just do as you're told."

When she got like this there wasn't anything I could do but

give in, so I slowly lowered my sweats again and bent over. Head up, eyes forward, scanning the horizon for unwanted company, I could feel her buggering me with her fingers. I started grumbling about *now not being the time* and *work to do* and *other locations* until I felt her fingers withdraw. I started to stand up. She pushed me back down with a firm hand to my lower back. "I'm not done yet. Cool your fucking jets." It was then I felt the big, stainless steel plug go in—the one with the wide, flat base and the tiny neck. The one I couldn't push out, at least not easily. "There, now, you can stand up."

"What the fuck, Dawn?"

"Oh, stop grousing. We're wasting time. Pull up your pants and let's get to the next location."

I stood up, feeling the plug seat itself inside me, and pulled my sweats over my half-hard cock, then looked back to see her packing up her beach bag and heading up the rise to the car. It was then I realized I was in for it. I should have known better than to agree to bring Dawn along to scout locations.

Actually, I'm used to running around with a plug in my ass. Dawn often enjoys plugging me and sending me out on errands, so it didn't take much time to get used to the feeling. I followed her up and settled into the driver's seat with a little groan and we were off to the second stop, a field under the Throgs Neck Bridge.

We pulled the car to the side of a deserted road. As we got out and began to walk toward the bridge supports, we were bombarded with mosquitoes and gnats. The ground was really marshy. I decided this wasn't a location I needed, crossed it off my list and we headed back to the car. Our next stop was an abandoned manufacturing plant.

We parked between two buildings, the old, dirty windows on one side of the alley reflecting the graffiti and brick walls of the building on the other side. I took lots of pictures and made notes about how to get there and ideas for filming. Farther back, there was a secluded area with rusting machinery. I was taking pictures when I felt Dawn's hand at my waistband. "What now?" I asked.

"Don't worry about it. Just keep working. I'm starting to get a little hungry. Didn't you say we'd have lunch on City Island?" She snaked her hand inside my sweats and pulled my cock and balls out the top.

"Jesus Christ!" I swore.

"There's nobody here but the pigeons. Relax, Harris."

I looked down to see what she was doing just as she produced a rubber cock ring. She put it in her mouth and began to stroke my cock. I watched as it expanded and lengthened and knew where she was going with this but was helpless to do anything about it. Actually, that's not true. I'm bigger than she is and I could have easily overpowered her and manhandled her to the ground and...yeah, see, powerless to stop her.

Once I was hard, she withdrew the cock ring, dripping with her saliva, and forced my cock and balls through. I reached for my pants and she said, "Wait. One more thing." I must have groaned because she smacked my hard cock and told me to be quiet. She produced a roll of surgical tape and taped my now straining cock to my abdomen, then wrapped the tape around my hips, trapping my cock against my body. "This way, no one can tell you're hard." She pulled my pants back up and over the top of my cock. She traced the elastic of the sweatpants, where it met my skin. "But I only have to reach a little way in and"—she pushed her finger inside the waistband, scraped her nail against the stretched head of my cock and I jumped. Then she ran the tip of her finger through the precome. "Yeah, just like that.

"Did you take pictures of all those machines? Let's see what's around the other side of the building."

"I don't know if I can walk."

"Sure you can. Let's go." And she was off down the road.

I waddled behind her until I got used to the feeling of my cock being bound. When I caught up to her I said, "You know, you could have used the belt with the cock cuff."

"Nah, too much work lacing you into it. Today is all about stealth and speed. After all, you never know when we might run into people."

I shuddered at the thought. A few more pictures and we headed to the car. "I don't know if I can drive like this. I don't even know if I can sit down."

"Don't be ridiculous, of course you can sit down. If you think you'll be too distracted to drive, I'll take over. We have one more site to look at before lunch, right?"

We heard voices and got to the car just as a group of guys came into view. I didn't want to know what they were doing in this desolate location so I quickly slipped behind the wheel and Dawn got into the passenger seat and we took off.

"See, I knew you could drive."

"Yeah, but the seat belt is killing me."

"Poor baby. Turn left at the stop sign." She guided us to the next location; this one was a maze of half-torn-down stone and brick walls with no roof. I loved it immediately. Loved the light coming from above and through the holes in the walls. I loved the rusted girders and twisted rebar. This would be a great location for the confrontation between the killer and the detective. My mind was on my work as I snapped photos and took notes. I was completely oblivious to what Dawn was doing until she began to pull my pants down again. "Got everything you need?"

I froze. "Um, yeah, I guess." I felt surgical scissors slide under the tape by my cock.

"This'll do," she said. She cut my cock free and stuffed the tape in her bag. "Wouldn't want to litter. Stroke your cock for me, baby. Now, bend over and brace yourself against the wall. Keep playing with yourself. That's right." I felt her fingers at the base of the plug. "Deep breath, Harris, and push. You know how to do it." She tugged hard and my sphincter retracted as the bulb of the anal plug was expelled.

I started to rise again, cock in hand and still hard when she pushed me back down and I felt something else press against my gaping anus. "Always in a rush. I wouldn't want to waste this beautifully opened hole," she said as I felt the dildo slide in easily. "Bend your knees, baby, and raise your ass just a little. Yes, that's it," she said as she began to slowly fuck me. Somewhere along the line, while I'd been taking pictures, she'd slipped into her strap-on harness. Or maybe she'd been wearing it all along, under her dress. Maybe all she had to do was insert her cock.

She began to fuck me in earnest. "Play with yourself, Harris. I'll let you know when you can come." Her hands were on my hips as she thrust against me, burying her cock up to its silicone balls. She started with an even rhythm of hard, slow strokes but soon sped up, fucking the living shit out of me. "Grab your balls, baby, and pull down. You know what I want."

I groaned as I pulled on my balls. They were extra sensitive from the vise of the cock ring. I braced myself as best I could as she pounded into me. I felt like I would burst right out of the ring when I felt her arm reach around, up under my shirt, her fingers stroking and teasing my nipples. Then she pinched one. I knew this combination well from past experience: her in my ass, my own hand pulling steadily down on my balls while she played with my nipples. This would push me over the edge in no time. A quick jack of the cock and...

"Oh god, please, may I, please Ma'am, please Dawn, can I please," I begged.

"Yes, baby, you can come," she replied. She almost said it too late as a string of semen shot from my cock to splatter against the wall in front of my face. "Ooh, good boy," she said, driving her cock into me three more times as I collapsed, shoulder against the wall.

I heard the sound of a plastic zipper bag and then she pulled out of me. Less than a minute later, she was taking the cock ring off and pulling up my pants. I turned around and she was standing there like nothing had happened. I looked into the beach bag and saw a plastic bag containing her cock, shiny with lube, and my stainless steel plug. "I'm starving," she said. "How far is it to City Island?"

We made it back to the car. She drove. I managed to give her the directions but it was difficult to pay attention, worrying about what she had planned for after lunch and the Staten Island locations.

WELL LIT

Sara Taylor Woods

Talia likes to sit at my feet when she reads. I've never told her to do it, never even asked her. When pressed, she blushes prettily and avoids my eyes and won't answer me. And really, I like it—the warm, soft curve of her rib cage pressing against my leg, the familiar vanilla smell of her, the way her fingers trace senseless designs on the top of my foot.

Tonight, my own book lies in my lap, forgotten. I can't take my eyes from the graceful slope of her neck and shoulder, how her head tilts, how her fingers creep absently to her collarbone, to her ear. The Christmas tree throws blinking red and blue shadows from the next room, dusting over her dusky skin like snowdrifts.

I want to replace her fingers with mine. Those lights with my mouth.

She arrived this afternoon clutching a brass menorah and a box of candles, her chin stuck out like I was going to laugh at her. She came in and we ordered Chinese and when the sun went down, she lit four candles, said the blessing and set the menorah in the front window of the dining room. I went to the recliner, barefoot and shirtless, and she settled at my feet.

The haphazard shadows from those guttering candles join the Christmas lights painting the walls. I run my hand over Talia's hair, my fingers wrapping around the back of her neck. I squeeze, and she shivers, laying her head on my knee.

I say, "What are you reading?"

Beat. "Hmm?"

I grin and pinch her earlobe. She jumps, but I can feel her smile against my leg. "What," I say again, "are you reading?"

"Herman Wouk."

"Heavy." My hand goes back to her hair, and she rubs her cheek against my knee like a cat. "Put it down," I say, "and come up here."

She doesn't even bother with a bookmark, just lets it slide onto the floor, then turns and climbs into my lap. She hikes up her sweatpants and straddles my hips, but doesn't touch me. Just watches me. Just waits.

"I got you something," I say.

"What?" she says. "You said—"

I tap her bottom lip. "I said you shouldn't get me anything. I didn't say I wouldn't get you something if I felt like it. And I felt like it."

She retreats in protest. "Sean—"

I grab her chin and kiss her; her reaction is immediate, electric. Her hips grind against me, the fingers of one hand brushing my collarbone. My cock is suddenly, painfully hard. I grab her hands and pull them behind her back, hold her wrists with one hand. I push up against her, fisting my free hand in her hair. My lips on her throat, her chest, and she's panting, her pupils huge and unfocused in the flickering darkness. I could let go of her hands—they'd stay as effectively as if they were bound.

That knowledge—that I can mold her, arrange her limbs and her mind, and that she'll stay, holding the shape I want like wet clay—is intoxicating. When she's like this, her eyes shining and distant, her breath ragged, the temptation to see how far I can push is nearly overwhelming.

I like to watch the struggle. The battle of wills. Often, that's enough.

It isn't tonight.

I let go of her wrists and tuck my hand under her ass. I stand up and she wraps around me like a summer night. She won't stop grinding against me, even in this precarious arrangement, and I pin her to the wall.

"Behave," I growl in her ear, "and I'll let you come tonight."

She whimpers, her bottom lip catching between her teeth.

"Are you going to behave?" I ask. "Or am I going to have to take you over my knee right here in front of the window?"

She squirms, but doesn't respond.

"Talia." I lean into her. "Answer me."

Finally, she nods, and I bury my face in her neck, my beard rasping against her skin, my teeth scraping along her throat. She tips her head back and something like a growl boils out of me. I carry her to the dining room table; the lights on the Christmas tree wink off, on, in patterns, bouncing off the mirror-black windows. My mouth has a mind of its own, dragging across her collarbones, down her sternum.

"Stand up." When she lets go, I step back and say, "When I come back, I want you naked, bent over that table. You understand?"

She nods.

When I step into the hallway, I can hear her scrambling to strip her sweats off, to lose the top. I want to watch, want to see the first smooth revelation of her skin, the warm brown of her nipples, the parentheses of her hips.

But I pull the plastic bin from the top shelf of the hall closet and grab the shopping bag from the floor. And when I return, I see Talia bent over the table, her long slender legs crossed at the ankle, trembling, hourglassing up to the perfect heart of her ass, and she's so fucking beautiful like this, waiting, I can't even breathe.

I swallow and drop my burden. The clatter makes her jump, and she lifts her head to look behind her. I raise my eyebrows, circling an index finger. Her eyes widen, and her face disappears behind the curve of her ass again.

I snort, amused at her dismay, and I grab her scarf from the hat rack. I come up behind her and slap her ass. She jerks and gasps, but she doesn't look back again. Her arms are stretched across the table, her cheek pressed against cool wood.

"I don't recall," I murmur, letting the fringe tickle the small of her back, "telling you to move. I think what I said was to be bent over this table. Isn't it?"

She doesn't say anything. I slap her ass again, pausing to admire the pink-and-white outline of my hand. I purse my lips, tracing my palm print with a fingertip.

"Isn't it?"

She nods and whispers, "Yes."

I walk my fingers across her skin, just skirting her pussy. Not touching it. "Yes...?"

She swallows and pushes her hips up into my hand. I give her a sharp swat. She backs off.

"Yes," she whispers, "Sir."

"Good girl." I run my hand down the curve of her ass, and she gives a feline little mewl. "Lift your head, baby." She does, and I wrap the scarf around her eyes, knotting it behind her head.

I fucking love this part: the visible shift in priorities, deciding
which of her remaining senses is the most important. The tightening of muscles, the parting and licking of lips. Breath quick,
hoarse. The runs of gooseflesh.

I pull out the string of Christmas lights from the plastic bin
and drop them on the table next to Talia. She jumps. I pinch the
back of her thigh. She squeaks. I grin.

"Spread your legs," I say. "Let me see you."

She unhooks her ankles, but doesn't spread them wide
enough. I know she's embarrassed—she's got her ass pointed
at the front window, and we can't lower the blinds, not until
the Hanukkah candles have gone out. She's got at least another
hour.

I squat next to her and run a hand up the inside of her thigh,
the tips of my fingers dragging in that space between lips and
leg. She shudders; even her inner thighs are wet.

"Don't make me tell you again," I murmur, "or I will tie you
to this table and leave you here all night."

Her feet inch apart. Almost there.

"You don't want my neighbor to see you like this when she's
walking those miserable little Scotties tomorrow morning, do
you?"

That does the trick, and she finally gets her legs right. I
smile and start pulling the lights from their plastic H-frame.
The frame fits neatly between her ankles, lashed into place with
braided wire.

Up one calf, draped along the line of her torso, looped
around her neck, back down the other side, winding down her
other calf. Under the table. Around her wrists.

I plug the lights in.

Her reflection in the window, limned in white lights, affects
me in a way I hadn't anticipated. "Look at me," I say, and I'm

alarmed at how dry and husky my voice is. We both know it's
stupid, that she can't see me, but she lifts her head anyway, her
nose pointing toward the sound of my voice. I run my fingers
over her forehead, smoothing out the hair caught under the scarf.
She leans into my hand, like she did when we sat reading, and
I catch a fistful of her hair, pulling her head back even farther.

Her breath saws in and out of her mouth, her pulse pounding
wildly in her throat.

I just hold her there for a moment, before I'm able to speak.
"I have your present."

She swallows, her throat working. I want to run my tongue
up the ridges of her trachea. I want to bite her, want to watch
her dissolve and run through my fingers. I want to mark her,
want to tell the whole fucking universe *hands off,* and I don't
want to use words.

"Sean?" Her voice is tiny in the blinking darkness. She's
going to protest again, and I cut her off, bringing my hand down
on her ass, my fingers spread. She whimpers, the table creaking
beneath her shifting weight.

"I did not give you permission to speak." I make a lot of
noise with the shopping bag; there's only one thing in it, but I
can't resist fucking with her. "I bought you something, baby.
Deal with it."

The vibrator is pretty tame, all things considered. But when
she told me that she'd never owned one before—never even used
one—I had no choice. And now that I'm staring at it, I find it
strange we've been playing for all these months without one.

So much we haven't done. So much I want to do. Her body is
stretched out, taut, vibrating like a violin string. I lick my lips,
untangle my fingers from her hair.

"Do you remember what you said about sex toys?"

Her head cocks, tilting maybe an inch to the right. If she

could see, she'd be looking into the left corner of the ceiling. Finally, she shakes her head.

"You said that buying a sex toy is a commitment. More than a safeword. Because it's got one use. It's dedicated to fucking. And *that* makes you feel dirty. Not the bruises I've left on you." I run my fingers along the tender boundary between her thigh and ass. "Not when I made you come in your aunt's guest bathroom halfway through Thanksgiving dinner." I smirk. "Do you remember that? You were horrified. You were so fucking wet."

I dip a fingertip into her pussy, swipe up toward her ass. She moans, pushing her hips up to my hand, and her forehead thumps against the table.

I lean down and kiss her cheek, leaving my lips close to her ear. "You'll get your present. But if these lights go out"—I tap the wires around her wrists—"I'm switching to the belt."

She whines and tries to bury her face in her armpit.

She hates the belt. She loves the belt.

My fingers find her pussy again, and she jerks against my hand. She pushes back against me, and I pull my hand away, a gossamer trail stretching between her cunt and my fingers. It catches the blinking Christmas tree lights before it breaks. I lay into her ass, my hand cupped, a little upswing in my stroke. The pops of flesh echo in the little room.

Thirty seconds in, her ass is pink and red all over and she's squirming. I stop and push two fingers back into her.

God*damn*—the *noises* she makes launch straight from my brain to my dick, and I can barely keep my balance.

I do it three more times, spanking her and finger-fucking her, shortening the intervals each time, and she's writhing, shaking under my hands, willing to fuck anything, willing to do anything as long as it brings her relief.

I press the vibrator against her before I switch it on. I don't want her to have time to process the noise, to know what's coming. I don't want her to be able to prepare for it.

When it comes on, her hips twitch so violently the whole table moves. "Jesus," she pants. "Fuck. Sean—"

"Careful," I murmur, dragging the little toy up to her clitoris. She shudders, lacking breath to even curse me again. "Shame to unplug the lights."

The orgasm that rocks her seems to take her by surprise, her voice cracking hoarse. She's trying to dance away from me, but I keep the vibrator pressed against her, my palm on the small of her back. "Hold still," I growl. She whines, and I slap her thigh. "Hold. Still."

She does, and the next orgasm comes less than a minute later.

"Sean," she pants, "please—"

I lean down and bite her ass. She jerks against me, her legs trembling, every muscle drawn tight like piano wire.

"Please, Sean, what?" I ask.

She doesn't answer, but I'm willing to forgive her when I see her fingers curl into tense fists, and she comes again, bucking against my hand.

"Fuck," she mutters.

She's leaning away from me, and I wrap my fingers around her hip to pull her back into position. "Please, Sean, *what*?" I ask again.

She keeps moving away from me, trying to avoid the vibrator. Even a half-dozen sharp swats—the last one grazing her shining cunt—don't keep her where she's supposed to be.

"Talia," I snap. "Quit trying to pull away from me. I'll tell you when you're done."

"I can't." She swallows. Licks her lips. "Please. I can't. I'm sorry."

"You can, baby." My voice is as soft as hers. "Give me one more."

She does. This one takes longer than the other ones, but it's a hell of a lot bigger. Her whole body clenches and curls up, and when her fisted hands jerk up from the table, the string of lights goes dark.

For a moment, we're both silent, immobile. Processing what just happened.

I unbuckle my belt.

It slides out of its loops with its own eagerness. I switch off the vibrator and drop it on the table, then walk around to the other side to squat down in front of Talia.

The look on her face is priceless—the belt scares the shit out of her, and works her up like almost nothing else we do. I suspect it falls into the same category as sex toys, but she won't admit it.

"Sean," she whispers. "Please."

I know what she wants—for me to fuck her—and, for what it's worth, I do, too. My cock is straining against my jeans, and I know that when I finally get inside her, when I feel her satin heat wrap around me, I won't be worth shit.

"No," I say. "No more free passes. No more begging. I told you not to unplug the lights, and I told you the consequences."

Her brow wrinkles over the top of the scarf, and she sucks her lower lip into her mouth, contrite. It's impossible to explain to her why I'm doing this. Why I have to.

Because I can't handle it when you pull away. Because I can't think straight when you avoid my hand, and because I love you, god, so much, and when you pull away from me, it hurts.

"Okay?" My voice cracks. I clear my throat. Try again. "Okay?"

She nods. "Okay."

I want to kiss her, want to feel her lips give against mine, her forehead against mine. I want to fuck her and carry her upstairs and spend the rest of our lives in bed, her shoulder tucked against my ribs, one soft hand spread like a star over the beat of my heart.

I stand up, folding the belt in half, and walk around the table again. She's swaying. I lay my palm on the small of her back, and she stills, but when my fingertips brush her ass, she gasps. Her heat sears me, and I can't stop my hand fanning over the spread of one cheek.

I'm tempted to wring another orgasm from her. Just because I can.

"You are so goddamn beautiful." I hadn't meant to speak out loud; my words fall like snow around us, piling up in drifts, soft, heavy. I trace a bright welt, and she shudders, but not from pain. "Look at you," I murmur. "So patient." I pinch her inner thigh, my knuckle brushing against her clit; she jerks away from me again.

My hand falls hard against her ass, flat-palmed and spread-fingered, not bothering to aim for the fleshy part. She gasps, the noise almost a sob, but she doesn't try to evade it. She isn't afraid of the pain. She's afraid she's going to come again.

She's afraid I'll make her.

I twist my fist in her hair, pulling her head back, and push two fingers into the heat of her cunt. She rises off the table like a parabola, panting.

"Do not," I growl, "pull away from me. This"—I twist my fingers inside her, letting the belt scrape against the raw flesh of her ass—"is mine. Do you understand me? You'll come if I want."

She's stopped resisting. She's so good at absorbing the pain, but that isn't what I want. I want her to take everything I give her. I want her to drink it down, to metabolize it.

"Talia." I pull my fingers out of her and bring the belt down across her ass, once, twice. My fingers plunge inside her again, and her hips jerk against the table, the skid of its legs a startling stutter in the silence.

Her throat works, muscles straining around the arch of her neck.

"I need to break you of this habit." I want to smooth her sweaty hair from her forehead and kiss her, but I don't. I pull my fingers out of her again and let her hair go, let that hand slide down her spine to the small of her back, relishing the perfect curve of bone, the play of muscle, the softness of her skin.

Six strokes, the perfect gradient of purple to red to pink lining her ass. She takes them without a sound, just hard breaths and tight fists.

But when I say, "Four more. Then you're going to come again," she turns her head to me, mouth open to plead. I press her face to the table and the belt comes down again. The noise it rips from her is almost a scream.

Three more, and I yank the lights from her, kick the frame from between her feet, and scoop her up in my arms. I grab the vibrator and carry her into the living room, pulling the scarf from her eyes as I walk. I lay her down on the carpet and she winces, the pile rough against her tender skin. I pull her hands over her head, then wind the scarf around her wrists, not bothering to tie it. I don't need to. Her eyes are wide and glassy, and when I wrap my hand around her throat, they flutter shut.

"No," I say. "Look at me."

When she does, I unbutton my jeans and pull out my cock. "I'm going to fuck you." I feather my fingers across her cunt, making her moan. "You're going to come on my cock, because that's what I want. And you're going to be looking at me when you do it."

She hesitates. Nods, her lower lip between her teeth.

I growl. I want to bite her. But I just say, "Good girl."

I push into her, and for a second, the whole world stops, shut down by the smooth heat of her clenching around me. Her jaw drops open, and her short, sharp gasp almost makes me come. I swallow against it, shaking—I know I won't last long, but I need to make it a couple of minutes, at least.

One stroke, two, and I feel a little more anchored to the planet. I pick up the vibrator and switch it back on. Her lower lip's between her teeth again, and I lean down, get right in her face.

"You keep biting that lip, you're going to give me ideas."

She whimpers, but I keep my hand on her throat when I curl down to suck a nipple into my mouth. She arches under me, and I bite her, pressing the vibrator between us.

She yelps, squirming. I squeeze her throat.

"Nowhere to go, baby," I whisper. She's panting, looking everywhere but at me. I'm scaring her, and it has nothing to do with my grip on her neck. "Come for me. Give me one more."

I can feel her tensing beneath me, trying to push another out, but she's still not looking at me. I let go of her throat and slap her cheek. She gasps, her cunt spasming around me.

"Talia. Look at me."

She does, finally.

"Sean," she pants. "I can't."

"Yes, you can." I pinch her nipples. "You'll do it for me." The carpet and the open zipper of my jeans are scraping her ass, and I know she likes it. I sit back on my heels, dragging her with me by the hips. Her legs fall open. Short thrusts, but deep, the vibrator pinned between us. I slap the insides of her thighs, hard enough to leave bright white handprints.

"Come on, baby."

I grab her throat again, and suddenly, I can see it: her whole body tensing, her hands curling into fists above her head, her hips tilting up toward me. Her body bows, trembling, then all at once, she shouts something incoherent and stretches out, her spine arching off the carpet. I have to hold on to her hips to keep her from rolling away. The way her pussy pulls at me, fluttering pulses running along the length of my cock, pushes me hard, and, squeezing her hips hard enough to leave bruises, I come, too.

I slide out of her and before I've even caught my breath, I kick my jeans off. I free Talia's wrists and pull her into my lap, my back against the couch. I grab the blanket from the sofa and wrap it around her. Her head rests on my shoulder, and I kiss her forehead, my arm curled around her.

She looks up at me, her eyes pink and puffy, her face streaked with tears. My chest is hot, tight, like there's not enough room for everything in there, and I smile down at her.

She says, "I love you."

I kiss the top of her head. "I love you, too, baby."

She smiles, broad and relieved, like she hadn't been sure how I'd respond, and snuggles down against my chest. I lean back into the couch, one arm around her, the other in her lap. She plays with my hand, running cool fingertips over my skin.

When she speaks again, her voice is thick, sleepy. Just a whisper. "Merry Christmas, Sean."

I lace my fingers with hers and bring her hand up to my lips. I kiss her knuckles, her fingertips. "Happy Hanukkah, baby."

A SOUNDPROOF ROOM WITH A VIEW

Leigh Edward Gray

W e're going to Brooklyn."

"What's in Brooklyn?"

"A soundproof room. You know, in the boroughs, no one can hear you scream."

She had known there was an apartment with a soundproof room in Brooklyn that he took girls to, but knowing she was now the girl made her imagination run wild. Was it a basement apartment? She had seen a scene or two by this time, but somehow she always imagined them in a dungeon.

"I hardly think I'll be screaming."

"Never say never. You *did* say not to go easy on you."

Right. Why had she said that again? It was right after he had sent her a checklist of all the things they could do together, some predictable, some she had never heard of, some that sounded downright scary. There was a place for her safeword, a place for names she was uncomfortable with, a place for hard and soft limits in case the checklist wasn't extensive enough. She had seen doctors with less thorough paperwork. She worried that all the negotiations might take the fun out of things, but seeing how seriously he took it was exciting. She had been spanked, tied up and blindfolded before, but this wasn't going to be a few love taps before lovemaking. This would be the real thing, the real submission that she had longed for.

She never thought she'd be doing it with her ex, however. The relationship was over, in the ground for going on three years now, but the friendship had pulled through. She had been there to see his progress from first-timer to self-assured dominant, though she had missed the signs at first. He was careful with her, once they were just friends. She hadn't realized just how careful until she'd seen him with someone else.

After some cajoling, some whining, some reasoning and some scheming, she finally convinced him to take her to one of the parties he kept so secret. She wasn't sure if it was the whip or if it was him holding the whip that was so exciting, or maybe just the cries and marks of the girl in front of him. But she hadn't even been able to wait twenty-four hours before she asked him. Stumbling over her words, blushing like she hadn't since the mid-'90s, she had only been able to ask if he would do "all that stuff" to her. That had gotten her the checklist.

Less than an hour after she sent it back, he told her—no asking for him—to meet him for dinner. It was a strange meal. She didn't know if she was to act normally or to be submissive. Now, in the car outside her building, it was a relief to bring it out in the open.

"So I'll be picking you up at ten tomorrow morning. You're going to be wearing a collar when we're together in the room. Would you like to see it?"

"Okay."

He reached into the back and retrieved a black leather collar, on the heavy side, with a ring at the front and a serious buckle at the back. "Do you want to try it on?"

She licked her lips, looking around at the dark street. It was empty, but... "Here?"

"Yes, here."

She eyed the collar again. "Okay." She leaned forward and felt the collar at her neck a moment later, tightening as he fastened it in place. "Not too tight?"

"No."

His hand stayed on her neck, rubbing just above the collar in a slow stroke. "Does it feel good?"

"Yes."

"Good. You'll be wearing this tomorrow. When I put it on, we'll begin. When I take it off, we're done. Three rules when you're in the collar: one, you will call me 'Sir.' Two, you will stay quiet unless I tell you to speak. Three, you will not come unless I tell you to. Do you understand?"

"Yes."

"Good. If you break any of those rules, you *will* regret it. We won't do anything you didn't say was okay or anything we didn't talk about. If you need to stop or take a break, you'll say your safeword. What is your safeword?"

"Pineapple."

"And you'll say it when?"

"Whenever I need to stop or take a break."

"Good. If you can't speak, you're going to snap three times. Understand?"

"Yes."

"I don't think I'll need to gag you. You'll learn to be quiet and I bet if I tell you to keep your mouth open for me, you will. Right?"

She looked down. "I can try."

He touched her face, forced her eyes up. "Well, don't worry. We'll find out very quickly how obedient you can be. And if you can't be good, I'll just have to punish you until you improve. I have plenty of ideas of what I'm going to do with you and a soundproof room to do them all in. I suggest you get a good night's sleep," he said, reaching around and undoing the collar.

"Do we have to wait until tomorrow? Can't I just stay with you tonight?"

"No. We'll start tomorrow like I just said."

"I'm not gonna be able to sleep tonight."

"Sure you will. Just go up and think about what I said and make yourself come five or six times. You should probably enjoy it while you can because you're really gonna be working for it tomorrow."

"You're really making me go up."

"I'm not saying it for my health."

"This is annoying," she grumbled as she got out of the car.

"You know, tomorrow you're going to wish you'd sucked up to me a little more."

"That's okay. I'm betting it wouldn't make a difference. I'm betting if I begged, it would just make you harder."

"You kiss your mother with that mouth?"

"I don't know what I'll be doing with it soon."

"Thanking me, if you're good." He started the car. "Now go up and go to bed. Don't think I won't be able to tell if you stayed up late."

"Okay, okay. Tomorrow morning. Ten."

"Sharp," he added as he pulled away.

Her first thoughts upon waking were of the day ahead. It was nine. The hour she had to prepare seemed entirely too long, but by the time she got dressed, it was almost ten. She settled on a short, dark-gray dress with black stockings that came just up over the curve of her knees, and heeled shoes she could stand in for a few hours. She did her makeup, having no idea if it would be on long. Should she wear waterproof mascara? Might she really *cry*?

The buzzer rang at ten; it was too late to have second thoughts. She could always say *pineapple*. She always had *pineapple*. Even if she kept it in for as long as she could.

Getting into the car was normal. He handed her a cup of coffee. It stayed normal halfway to Brooklyn. He even let her pick the radio station. But as they got closer, he turned it off and said, "Are you done with that coffee?"

"Yeah."

"Are you ready to put the collar on?"

They were stopped at a red light. She looked around. Traffic was sparse but there. "Right now?"

"Yes, right now."

"Okay."

He opened the armrest and took it out. He must have been planning this. "Come here." The light was still red. A car pulled up next to them. It was on the driver's side, but she still ducked her head so her hair hid her face. When it was buckled, the car seemed more quiet. He seemed more quiet. The very streets around them looked different.

"Are we almost there?" He didn't answer, didn't even look over. "Hmm?" Then she realized—she was talking. And she hadn't said "Sir." Two strikes and they hadn't even gotten through the intersection. "Sorry. Sir."

"It's another mile. Just look out the window." It was another five blocks before he said, "We're not having sex today." She didn't turn but she knew he could see her tense up. "I think that's a little too intense for your first time. Is that okay?"

"Will it change your mind if I say no?"

"No."

"Okay then."

"Okay. Still ready to go? This is the place."

"Yeah." She looked at the dash instead of his eyes.

"It's eleven now. Still think you can make it till three?"

Was that how long she had said she could make it—*four hours*? Who had she been kidding? She hoped he would factor in her overconfidence. "Four hours might have been ambitious."

"Might have been. Get your bag and follow me. A few steps behind, mind you."

She stood next to the car with her bag while he fed the meter a few dozen quarters. He had his own bag as well, the one she knew contained all his toys. She kept her eyes on it while she followed him, three steps behind, into the building. Immaculate lobby, thankfully without a doorman, then a nice, quiet elevator where he touched the back of her neck just above the line of the collar. Two doors to the right. She left her bag at the door as instructed and followed him through one of the closed doors. Once it closed behind them, she could tell the room was soundproof. You'd never know there was a busy Brooklyn street right below them.

The room was not a dungeon, not by a long shot. It could have been a graphic design studio. Big, tinted windows let light stream in. There was a mini-fridge and a couch and a little table with a vase of wildflowers tastefully arranged on it. There was also a lot of scary-looking furniture, stocks and wooden horses and leather benches. There were hooks in the ceiling, some just in the beams and some on a pulley attached to a crank on the wall. One had a rounded end. She knew what that was for. There were a few hooks in the floor as well, quite a few—enough to tie someone down to the floor and barely leave them an inch to breathe.

He told her to stay put and for a few long moments, she knew only that he was moving behind her. She jumped when his hands landed on her shoulders and raked down her back and up to her hair. Gently running his fingers through it, soft and slow. "You look very nice today."

"Thank you, Sir."

"Did you think that would get you extra points?"

"No. I just wanted to look nice for you, Sir."

"That's very sweet. I hope you stay that sweet all day."

Then the hand in her hair turned a lot less gentle and jerked her forward, so hard that she stumbled and brought her arms up before she could think twice. "Arms down," and he waited until they were at her sides before he pulled again, all the way across the room and under the hooks. He let go with a push that almost made her trip again. She looked up at the hooks, then over to him. He was leaning against the wall, the picture of cool. He had taken his jacket off and wore boots, jeans and a thin, white T-shirt with the sleeves rolled up. The bag sat next to him.

"Lose the dress." When that was off, he said, "Lose the bra. The underwear can stay for now." She hadn't thought about how strange it would feel to take her clothes off in front of him again. When they were in a pile on the ground next to her, he told her to kick them aside. "Put your arms in front of you."

Out came the leather cuffs. They weren't that tight. Then he pulled one of the hooks down. "Arms up." The chain went over the hook. They were a little tighter now. Still not so bad. Then he went to the wall and started to turn the crank. The hook inched its way up to the ceiling and took her with it until her arms were pulled tight and her heels almost came off the ground. She could feel the strain start in her wrists, then shift down through her arms, her back, her hips, all the way to her feet. "Legs apart." That put her on her toes.

He went to the bag and pulled out his first selection. "Recognize this?" he asked, holding up the hairbrush. She did, it was *her* hairbrush, but she couldn't imagine how it got there. "You left it at my apartment about two months ago. I've told you several times to take it home with you. You'll probably never want to see it again after this."

He held her in place with one arm around her waist and starting swinging. There were no starter taps, and, as she quickly found out, a hairbrush could really *hurt*. He did one side, then the other, not skimping on the thighs, and even making her stand on one foot, wobbling like crazy, so he could get the tender insides.

"Well," he said, after enough strikes that she felt like every inch of her skin was burning and located on her ass. They were both breathing a little hard. "That's one shade down. Let's see how many more we can get in. But these are in my way," he said, tugging up the back of her underwear.

He went around her to the bag and took out a pair of sharp, shiny scissors. "Relax," he said, coming closer. "They're just for cutting these off." She still jumped when the blades pressed against her skin. He cut fast and clean at each hip and pulled them away from her body.

"What do you think?" he asked, holding them up so she could see the wet spot. "Should I gag you with them?" She knew better than to speak. "Come on, open your mouth." He moved them closer and she couldn't help shrinking away. He pulled her forward with a jerk on the collar. "Open your mouth or I swear to god you won't close it for the next three hours."

She squeezed her eyes shut and stuck her tongue out. "Beautiful." She felt his fingers trace her lips and she thought she might taste them but he said, "I changed my mind. I want to hear every noise you make." He went to the crank and let her down a little, enough that she could feel the sensation seep back into her arms.

Her flesh burned and throbbed when he came over and gave her ass a hard squeeze. She twisted in her bonds until he grabbed her and held her still. "I don't think I've ever seen this color on you. I'd call this two shades."

He let her go and went back to the bag, pulling out a monstrosity of thick wood, a paddle with a braided strip down the middle that left welts. She had always wondered if you could actually *feel* the braid. She tried to focus on it for a moment but the explosion of pain upon impact wiped away thought and it was all she could do to stay standing. She could certainly feel the braid *afterward*.

He let her down and took the cuffs off. She couldn't stop a cry when her arms fell to her sides. "Did that hurt? Don't worry, they're going the other way now." He pulled them behind her back and bound her elbows, then her wrists. Her chest was forced up and out. She expected him to touch her then, hoped for it, but all he did was bend her over a little and pick up the cane. She had been spanked. She had never been *caned*. But she had seen cane marks.

"You look scared," he said, bringing it down across one of the braid marks. It cut an arc that felt different from everything else; it shot straight through the ache with a sting that took her breath away. She found that she *did* cry, and shake, and scream, all before they even got to ten.

When he pushed her to her knees, she was just relieved that the cane was gone. When she heard his zipper, she was relieved to be back on familiar ground. She happily opened her mouth when instructed. But this wasn't what she was used to. This wasn't her giving a blow job. This wasn't her doing anything except keeping her mouth open while he fucked it.

He held her in place with one tight grip in her hair and one equally tight grip at the back of the collar, pulling it around her throat until she was straining for breath. With her hands bound, she could do nothing but take it, and he told her she took it beautifully, without a fight, without fear. Not even when she grew dizzy, her mind racing as she wondered whether he would let her pass out, and just what *was* the limit on breath play—not even then did she struggle.

Finally, he let go of the collar and the massive breath she drew in was immediately lost when he filled her mouth with his come, holding her in place against him. Some splashed over her breasts when he pulled out. She didn't move when he stepped back, still on her knees, mouth open and dripping, eyes closed. It was a long few moments before she looked up. He stood over her, cleaned up and impassive once again. She shuddered to think what she probably looked like.

"That was very good," he said, running a hand through her hair. It tingled and warmed her all the way through after all the pulling, feeling like some luxurious reward. "Are you wet?"

"Yes, Sir."

"I bet you'd be touching yourself if you could. Would you be making yourself come right now if I let you?" He bent down and ran a hand up her thigh, stopping just at the top and giving a little squeeze.

"Yes, Sir," she breathed out. She kept her eyes trained on the floor in front of her, on his leather boots. Her focus must have been a little too intense, because he moved away and came back with the little wooden chair from the corner and sat down. He moved one foot forward and waved a hand. "Go on, then."

"Sir?"

"On the boot if you want it so bad."

She eyed the boot. As she would many times with increasing

awe over the coming months, she thought, *He really* is *a sadist.* She must have taken a moment too many because he moved forward, faster than she was ready for, grabbed her and pulled her close. She almost fell over, the unstoppable need to catch herself meeting the immovable force of her hands bound behind her back. He didn't let her fall.

"Listen to me," he said, and she looked up at him before he had to correct her. "You *will* make yourself come, *yes*, on the boot, and you will fucking *thank me* for the privilege."

She knew her options were bad. She could either safeword and regret it, convinced that she could have taken more, could have taken anything when she was safe in her bed at home tonight. Or she would do it and never be the same. Never forget the mixture of gut-churning humiliation, the wonder at her body getting off while her mind was in turmoil, the heat in her cheeks, the tears and, above all, the burn driving her on, stoked by every spot of drool, every mark, every slap, consuming everything else. That was how someone was changed forever.

Pineapple. Pineapple. Pineapple.

"Yes, Sir."

She slowly inched forward on her knees, a fine tremble running through her, until she was flush against his leg, thighs spread apart and spreading wider as her hips jerked before she could stop them, grinding against the grain of the leather, too soft and too rough at once, too much of everything at once after so much nothing. She hid her face against his leg but that wasn't happening. He pulled her hair back until she was forced to look up. He didn't make her look at him; that was a kindness. But he did watch her. She could feel that even with her eyes squeezed shut.

She worked harder. She thought he was probably cruel enough to stop her right on the edge if she didn't go fast enough for his liking. Was he watching to see if he could catch her? Thank god she had her eyes closed. It seemed like forever with the strain in her shoulders, her knees on the floor, her arms useless and going numb behind her. But it wasn't in spite of these things that she came, but because of them. For a few hot seconds, there was nothing but sensations, so many at once, and she was screaming so loud she couldn't have had a thought if she wanted to.

Her body shook. She scraped her knees. She cried, *again.* And when it was over, the thoughts stayed quiet.

He looked pleased when she was done. He untied her arms and allowed her a few minutes to recover, curled up on the floor, before he asked, "Ready for more?" He had the bag.

"Yes, Sir."

"Good. All fours. Legs open."

And though she felt the humiliation of showing him her wet cunt, still aching for his attention, whatever he did with it, and felt the pain in her limbs as she got into position, the stinging burn that persisted in her ass, the shame when he made her clean his boots with her tongue—above all, she felt the sweet taste of satisfaction.

RECIPE FOR PUNISHMENT

Jacqueline Brocker

Four days of rain in their Cumbrian holiday cottage, and Katie was as horny as fuck. Their planned week of country-side walks and exploration had come to nothing as mud clogged the hillsides and water came down in thick sheets.

"Oh well," Will had said after the third day. "At least we can catch up on our reading."

Reading, Katie thought. *Fan-fucking-tastic.*

It was a complaint, Katie knew, that would strike most people as kind of funny—funny odd, not funny amusing. Because they'd had sex, every day, in fact. It was, however, of the incredibly basic thrust and grind variety that resulted in tiny exclamations from Will when he came and her sighing without satisfaction after he was done. He'd try to bring her to climax, finger rolling earnestly on her clit, but after the second time, she shook him off.

"Let it go, sweetie. We just need to wait."

He nodded, and a hint of fear dashed through his eyes. That was something, at least.

It was the waiting that was doing her in. She had to contain the bubbling urge to lash out; her shoulders were tense and she kept flexing her hands to stop them from giving Will an unprovoked smack on the ass. Will just kept smiling, as if happy that their holiday was ruined by the pissing rain and smattering of sleet.

But Katie couldn't punish him for his unrelenting optimism. That wasn't their style.

On the fourth afternoon, Katie decided to bake a cake, something to distract her and take her frustrations out without damaging anything in the cottage that wasn't their property. She added the vanilla extract with a heavy-handed sense of irony; it was meant to be the favored scent of strippers, the best in the world at getting men interested. Vanilla—something she really wasn't.

Will came into the kitchen when the batter was almost done and winked at her mischievously. Katie gritted her teeth, forcing a smile at him. The cocky look that danced across his face told her he knew he was annoying her, but to her chagrin, she couldn't gauge it more than that.

The games that they played had crept into their relationship like a slow-growing vine, curling and twisting into unexpected places until they were the common thread that bound them together. They'd learned the push and pull of each other over the years, and were still learning. And the thing that made the hairs on her neck stand up most in irritation was not knowing if he was plotting, or if he really was just acting like a five-year-old.

Katie picked up the bowl to give herself more traction for thickening the batter. She sensed Will behind her, but wasn't quick enough to stop him as he reached around her and dipped his finger into the cake mix.

Katie whipped around with the wooden spoon and waved it in his face. "Sod off!"

Will just chuckled, licked his finger, and stuck his tongue out at her.

She rolled her eyes and gave him a soft shove, but he tried to go for another dollop of mix. She grasped his arm, but he lunged past her. His hands knocked the bowl over, and it spun from Katie's hand. The batter splattered across the wooden floor before the bowl hit the ground and twirled like a dreidel. Katie and Will both watched as it took its rapid time before clattering against the fridge and coming to a stop.

Will's eyes flashed with horror and fear as Katie's face became a mask of rage. A mask, for she was furious, really fucking furious, but at the same time, joyous heat burst through her chest.

At last, she thought. Whatever he had intended when he entered the kitchen, now he'd given her permission to take charge.

The wooden spoon still in her hand, she pointed at the mess, her gaze fixed hard on Will.

"Clean it up."

Will winced but didn't move. She held the spoon like the flat edge of a knife, blunt and hinting at danger. And she knew exactly what he was thinking: W*as this it? Was it going to happen now?* He was trying to read her tone, figure out if her anger was burgeoning with threatening promise, or if she was genuinely pissed off.

Katie would have smiled, but that would have ruined her stern demeanor. Better to let him dangle.

"Clean it up *now*."

He nodded frantically. "Yes, sweetie."

She grabbed his chin with hard fingers. "Don't call me sweetie. Use my full name."

He swallowed, the underside of his chin undulating against her thumb. "Sorry...Catherine."

Katie could have petted him for that; the way he said it always made her feel regal. But she held back. Too soon—far too soon—for rewards. She let go and pointed back at the floor. He scurried to the sink, scooped up a scrubber and paper towel, and fell upon the batter.

As he cleaned, head down with deep, worried concentration, Katie washed the still sticky spoon. She dried it and opened the drawer of utensils. Out of the corner of her eye, she saw Will raise his head.

"Stay down."

He snapped back down and continued his furious scrubbing.

The drawer was full of tantalizing possibilities: egg whisk, tongs, serving spoons, metal skewers. Katie drew out one of the skewers and examined it with exaggerated interest, as one might inspect a dagger she intended to kill with, knowing Will was still trying to look up. When she heard his breath catch, she smiled and put the skewer back. Instead, she put the wooden spoon down and picked up the tongs.

"Are you done?" she asked without turning around.

"Almost, Catherine!"

"If it's not spotless you will lick up the rest."

The squeaky swipes of the towel became quicker. Katie tapped the tongs against the palm of her hand, slowly, listening to the sounds of him throwing things in the bin and washing his hands.

He became still. Katie turned around and found him with eyes cast to the floor, fidgeting hands clasping and unclasping in front of him. Katie swept her eyes over the now clean floor. It was better than before the spill. Good boy. But the cake would not be made now, and for that, Will still had to pay.

"Take your shirt off."

Will met her eyes, checking for confirmation. Impatient,

Katie smacked the tongs against her palm, the metallic clang sending Will's arms into a flurry of motion to pull off his jumper, followed by his long sleeved T-shirt. He left them on the kitchen counter, and goose bumps rose on his skin from the chill in the air. He wrapped his hands around his forearms and started rubbing up and down to warm himself.

Katie snapped, "Hands behind your back, for fuck's sake. A little cold won't kill you."

Chastised, Will mumbled, "Yes, Catherine." His hands dropped away, and in the cold air, his nipples hardened into two rounded pebbles.

Katie stepped closer to him, her pace stately and menacing. He was shivering, and she hoped it wasn't just from the chill. She slipped the tongs under his chin and raised it up so he was forced to look at her.

"You really are a bit of a brat, aren't you?"

Will's cheeks flushed pink. "I know."

Katie arched the tongs over his jaw, pressing lightly but enough to feel the bone. "That cake was your favorite."

Will nodded and gulped. Katie thought, *Good.*

She swept them up his cheek, aware of the softness of his skin, the structure of his cheekbones, the curve on the side of his eye socket, the delicate spot of his temple. She knew just what she could do to him, how it would be so easy to hurt him, and that he would cry out, but would not stop her.

Katie went to speak, but Will blubbered out, "I'm sorry, I'm so sorry! I was—"

Katie opened the tongs and swung them down his face to pinch his earlobe, and tugged. Will yelped, his body jerking downward, but he stopped speaking, and looked at her with wet eyes. *Oh Jesus*, Katie thought, and her clit began to swell.

"Shut up. Do not speak unless I tell you. You're sorry? You will be when I'm finished with you."

Will's teeth sunk into his lower lip. He was bracing against the pain in his ear, Katie knew, trying not to sob, but he nodded as much as he could. Katie snatched the tongs away.

"Stand up straight and look directly ahead. Don't look at me until I tell you to."

Will obeyed, his shoulders rolling back and settling down, his chest forward, his eyes fixing themselves on a spot behind Katie's head. His features were seemingly impassive, but his Adam's apple bobbed like a fish on a line.

She took the tongs and pressed the flat end against his left nipple. Will's chest rose and fell with a deliberate breath of anticipation. Katie's own body was on the edge of something glorious, and part of her wanted to jump off, grab him and fuck him until he screamed. But that would have ruined this new recipe. If they weren't to have cake, they would have this.

Now Katie opened the tongs, and with surgeon-like precision, took his nipple between the ends and squeezed. Will made a sound like a shivering puppy, fearful and unsure. All it took to make him howl was a sharp twist of Katie's wrist, and the nipple turned like a screw. Will's body jerked toward Katie. He remembered in time to stand up straight, but Katie twisted the nipple the other way, sending him off balance, making him cry out again, his body wrenching to the side to brace himself for it.

Katie's own nipples hardened beneath her jumper, and she exhaled to stop herself from just fucking him senseless.

She squeezed harder, and lifted it upward. Will arched back, rocking forward onto his toes, his mouth opening with a gasp.

"Oh god, oh god, oh god."

"No god here to help you," Katie snarled. She snatched the

tongs back and caught the other one. She twisted as she pinched down, and Will mewled. Katie paused for a moment, letting him pant, but she then tugged it to the right, then left, and then the same again several times over, her chest flushed with beating heat as Will kept moaning and keening.

Puppet on a string, Katie thought, and licked her lips.

Katie stopped abruptly and pulled the nipple toward her, the skin stretching white under the tongs. Will stumbled forward.

"You're sorry, Will?"

A frantic nod. "Yes! Yes, I'm so sorry."

Katie turned her hand gently to the left. "Good. Now, when I let go, you're going to face the pantry cupboard, drop your pants so I can see your arse, and brace yourself on it. Clear?"

"Yes, Catherine."

With a final twist, Katie let go, and Will sighed with delicate pain. He rushed to follow her command. As he did, Katie replaced the tongs with the wooden spoon.

Katie stared at his ass—a pale, unbaked cake, ready for the heat of the oven. Or rather, her beating hand. She cupped her hand around one cheek. It was so perfect and pert, still very pale, scarcely pink. She smiled, and dug her nails in, feeling his flesh between the nail and skin like dough.

"Now," she said, and laid the flat of the spoon on the place where his cheeks met in that sexy curve. "How many smacks do you think you deserve?"

Will shook his head. "I don't know, Catherine. I think you should decide."

Katie smacked the spot lightly. Will released a steady breath.

"Yes, you're right." She ran the spoon over the rounds of his cheeks. "Well, I think since that cake would have taken an hour to bake, then you should get a smack for every minute of that hour."

Will gasped. "Catherine—"

"Shut up. Sixty. I think that's perfect."

Will's breathing suddenly increased. His chest rose and fell rapidly. His voice was a whisper as he chanted, "Oh god, oh god, oh god," and Katie brought the spoon back to land the first one. Will whimpered.

"And you will count them. All of them. If you're quick, I'll be quick. If you're not, well, it will just last longer."

Will nodded. "One."

There was a tense calm in his voice, the utter need to remain in control, to sound each word for her as the spoon landed again and again. The sound of wood against flesh was a solid echo through the kitchen. She eyed his cheeks, shuddering and jiggling, and her lips parted as her inner thighs began to burn.

For the first ten he was steady, solid, his voice even. But then Katie sped up, and by twenty he was panting between each one. The longer words past that number though, with Katie's speed, his arse blooming redder and redder, came out gasped, strangled.

"Twenty-nine, oh god, ah! Thirty!"

He screamed at the halfway point, and Katie paused to slap each cheek with her hand. He started to say thirty-one, but Katie squeezed the back of his neck.

"No. That was my hand. Sixty with the spoon."

Will's head bent forward and let out a sob. "Please, Catherine, please..."

He wouldn't say *stop*. He would try everything else before that word would explode from his lips. She knew too well that he had too much pride, and the desire to be as strong for her rage as he could—but that didn't mean he wouldn't try.

"It's almost over. Remember, you could have been having cake now. So take the rest of it and remember you've been a naughty boy."

A sniff from Will. "Okay."

Katie raised the spoon back and began with renewed vigor. Will surged right to the pantry door, clawing at the lacquered wood, his eyes shut tight and his lips flapping in pain as he tried to form the numbers. The numbers fluctuated between whispers and shouts. His hand shot to his lips to bite down when Katie, at forty-four, made a small pause, then smacked down again so that he bit on his hand. He snatched it away, remembering the counting just in time.

"Forty-five. Oh fuck..."

Katie tsked, and grabbed his chin, wrenching him around to look at her.

"That's five more for swearing."

A wretched sob. "Oh please—"

She let go, and shoved his back so his body pressed to the pantry door. He groaned, and only now she saw the line of liquid down his cheek.

She hit the peak she always did. Words could be faked, cries and exclamations of pain exaggerated, and body movements part of the act. Tears, though...Katie raised her finger to the bottom of his cheek, catching the drop with her nail and sweeping it away along his skin.

Carefully brushing his chin, she said, her voice trembling, "Sweetie?" She hoped, *Christ she hoped*, he would hear the question behind her voice.

Will opened his tired, wet eyes, and gazed at her. Exhausted, yes, a little battered...but was he broken? Will took her hand from his chin, brought it between his legs. His cock was thick, hot and hard.

Relief filled her. Katie gave his dick a reassuring squeeze before setting herself back to begin again.

She took five to warm up, Will counting woodenly. At fifty,

Katie's arm swung back and she smacked him with a burst of grand energy. The final fifteen had him wailing, beating his fists against the wood, the tears flowing without shame, and when they reached sixty-five, Will sunk down the door, knees bent, sobbing.

Katie tore her clothes off and yanked him around so his back was against the door. His reddened cock was leaking, a single pearl hanging like a teardrop on the end. Between her legs the sticky wetness was thick and eager to flow.

Straddling his hips, she made him bend his knees a little, and urged the head of his cock to her entrance. And as she lowered herself, relishing the deliciousness of enveloping him, she said, "Now we both get dessert." He moaned in response.

She fucked him quickly, so fast that he grabbed her shoulders and slid to the floor. His teeth sunk into her shoulders, a bite of desperation. Her knees hit the tiles, but she didn't care, wanting only to hear him moaning, to have his arms around her, clinging to her as she rose and fell, while she covered him with her body, his cock buried in her. She rolled her hips in the precise way so the friction of her clit brought her to a fast, rapid orgasm, and as she threw her head back and screamed, beneath her, Will shuddered, calling out "Catherine" over and over as he came.

The kitchen spun around Katie. She dropped her head to his shoulder, panting, closing her eyes, hands on his back, feeling the sheen of slick sweat. Will mouthed at her neck, gasping followed by kissing, his hands running down her back, a reassurance he was okay. Katie rocked him, cradling him and silently thanking him for their shared release.

After a while, Katie stood up and wordlessly held her hand down to him. Will took it and swayed to his feet. They walked unsteadily through the cold kitchen and into the bathroom. Will started to run the bath, while Katie found the moisturizer. He bent forward and put his hands on the edge of the tub, while Katie ran the cool, cloudy liquid over his red buttocks.

He sighed and shivered. "I didn't actually plan to make you mad."

Katie curled her lip. "Could have fooled me."

He didn't respond for a few moments, allowing her to ease the moisturizer into his skin. When she was nearly done, he said, "I was a bit of sod, wasn't I?"

Katie chuckled—a tired but contented chuckle. "Yeah. But I've been waiting for the excuse, frankly."

"Mmm. Bloody cabin fever."

She paused, fingers on the small of his back. "You regret it?"

Will glanced at her over his shoulder. "I'm only sorry we won't be getting cake."

Katie grinned and reached forward to lightly cuff his cheek.

CRY TO ME

Skylar Kade

I perched at the end of our California King bed and waited. Every muscle was bowstring tight, eager and frightened for their dance to begin. I braced for the pain.

You asked for this. It was a harsh reminder.

As it had every time before, my safeword rolled around my tongue—sweet as a jawbreaker and just as likely to choke me. I swallowed it back anyway and threw my attention into the moment.

My lover, my Master, my husband entered the room, towing Chickadee along. We've called her that for so many years I almost didn't remember her name—something shrill and sharp that ill-fit her sweet, soft nature.

"The first time I asked for this," she cried.

"That kind of defeats the purpose," I'd told her. I was the one chasing tears. She was just, for temporary purposes, the implement of pain: a cane, a rod, a whip in woman form. Even so, after all the practice I'd given her, moisture lined her bruise-blue eyes.

He moved her onto the bed, facing me, on her knees. Chick-adee has the most open face and in this position every ounce of her pleasure would cut at me. He knew this, the sadistic bastard.

And he knew I'd like it.

I reached for her hand and came up inches short, in a rattle of chains. I'd forgotten about that, but now their cold, alien weight around my wrists and ankles seemed infinite.

My pulse beat against the manacles in a legato rhythm that synced up with Master's smooth, economical movements. In a sweep of his arms, he was as naked as we were. Waves of control rolled off him and his undertow sucked me down. I froze until he looked at me, then Chick.

Now the pain would begin. My breath whooshed out in a rattling sigh.

If human skin could shed like a snake's, maybe this itch would resolve itself. But no—when my skin stops fitting, when the pressure in my head threatens like an oncoming storm, we have to scrape me raw and clean.

Master kneeled on the bed and ran his hands up and down Chick's sides until she calmed. I'd make this up to her, as I always did. Until then, the guilt heaped weight onto my chest and pressed me closer to tears. But not close enough, not yet.

"Look what you've given me, *cara*. All this is mine, with your blessing." His hands dipped between Chick's thighs. Her needy moan rent the silent room.

His hands were on another woman while I was relegated to the spectator seats. My safeword flashed in the dark recesses of my head like a beacon, but I refused.

His lips—*mine, his lips and her body*—dropped kisses along her back. "She's so ready, I could take her right now, like this. Without you." The whole time, he stared at me. Taunting. Daring.

Just beyond the curve of Chick's ass, I could see his cock

jutting proudly upward. *Sadist*. The snarl almost left my mouth but I bit my lip instead.

He continued his verbal torment and said, "Is it lonely at the foot of the bed, *cara*?" His teeth sank into the flesh of her shoulder, leaving perfect little indents as she shuddered beneath him. I craved feeling that shiver run from her body to mine.

Expert that he was, Master played her body, complicated and resonant as a Steinway. He pressed the keys of her nipples and inner thighs and pussy lips until her moans played through the bedroom.

The bed dipped and Master's shadow shifted as he offered me his outstretched finger. Unsure what he wanted, I waited patiently—though inside I screamed to move—as he painted his finger across my lips.

"Taste her. She's so wet. Ready." My tongue flicked out. Chick did, as always, taste delicious. Pangs of longing roiled in my gut, my throat tightened, and I thought, *Maybe this time it could be easy.*

But no, crying was still something that had to be forced out of me, and damn did I ever need a good tear-fest about now. Thirty-five years, and this was the most pleasant of sadistic ways I'd discovered to elicit those cleansing tears.

Master paused, watching me. I knew he wanted to ask me to safeword; he didn't hate doing this like Chick did, but it still pained him. I gave a little shake of my head, a barely there smile of reassurance.

Those warm brown eyes I'd loved for decades hardened into granite. "Ready to cry for me, slut?" he asked me.

No, I wanted to scream, but that was just the fear talking. Instead, I nodded. "Yes, Master."

His musician's hands stroked once more down Chick's back. "Are you ready, darling?" he crooned.

My love for her swelled even as the green-eyed bitch in me ached to claw her eyes out. I reached for her, until the chains reminded me I was at their mercy until I broke.

I love you she mouthed at me. The words filed away the hard edges of my anger. Chick looked over her shoulder, showing me the lovely, youthful profile of her face. "Yes, Master."

In one thrust, he entered her. Chick shuddered and gasped; I knew exactly how good that first burning stretch felt. Master was thick enough that blow jobs had a serious learning curve, and Chick and I both disliked being warmed up too much before we took him. My pussy throbbed in jealous empathy.

He took up a pounding rhythm that wound me up with every beat. My heart pounded in time, screaming *mine*.

But not until I broke.

I dug fingers into my palms, even knowing physical pain wouldn't be enough. I thought of all the cases I'd won and lost this week in the Los Angeles public defender's office—the battered wives, the abused children, the men with PTSD—but if those were able to make me cry, I wouldn't be in this situation in the first place.

God, the looming tears strangled my throat but wouldn't dislodge.

Chick's cry of pleasure knocked the knot free from its wedge, closer to freedom. Closer to my fracturing.

Master's eyes closed and his fingers danced across Chick's body, scratching her back, tweaking her nipples, then finally dipping around her waist to strum her clit. I could see every-thing and hear her needy moans jump an octave when he hit the supersensitive spot at the top right side of her clit, the spot I loved to suck and nibble to make her come.

I could feel the moment they forgot about me, lost to their own pleasures. Loneliness, the one thing they'd promised I'd never again feel, crashed in and threatened to drown me. My vision swam on rising tears but they would not fall. And Master would not stop until I was bawling.

In retrospect, I regretted making him agree to that.

"Fuck, she is so goddamn tight." Master's lust-bright eyes locked on mine. His words scraped me raw. "I can feel her squeezing around me when I play with her clit. You wish you were licking her right now, don't you? But that's only for good girls, not bad sluts like you."

It hurt like a good, deep fucking. *Did I want to get closer, or pull away?* Neither—the chains answered that for me. I was good and trapped, stuck watching my lovers screw themselves to oblivion.

"Master, oh!" Chick's yelp, and the position of his hands pressing against her abdomen, told me he was bumping her G-spot. I knew that would make her come, which would push him over the edge.

And I'd be left wanting.

Through heavy lids, Chick looked at me. Her lips were swollen from her lip biting, a carryover from her more modest days when screaming out in pleasure was frowned upon. Usually it was endearing; now it teased me. I wanted to be nibbling her lips, swallowing her cries. "Lettie, please…"

Shit, she knew me. She saw what I needed. One tear trickled from the corner of my eye. *Not enough.*

"I'm so close, girl. Do you want to be stuck at the foot of the bed all night?" His words lashed at me, more painful in contrast to Chick's softness.

"Lettie, let go. I'll—" she gasped. Master's evil fingers had locked around her nipple and were pinching until Chick forgot her words. I knew that mind-numbing pleasure-pain. I ached for it now. Chick swallowed and grappled to continue. "I'll hold you."

A soft rainfall of tears now, rolling down my wet cheeks and dropping down onto my breasts. *Still not enough.* I looked down at the dove-gray duvet that we three had picked out together, just to see something other than my loneliness reflected in their pleasure, and my heart broke. All my self-doubt wiggled through the fissure and sucker-punched me in the gut until I couldn't breathe. Heaving, wracking cries shook my body but I made no sound.

Iron fingers clenched around my jaw. *Master.* He's still inside Chick, whose little fists were clenched around the duvet in that universal sign of sexual frustration. "Weep for me, slut." The jagged-edged command was followed by a sweet, tender kiss.

I cried like it was monsoon season in my heart and all that anxiety and self-doubt flooded down the river of my body. Clicks and clanks registered in the back of my mind but nothing made sense until I was surrounded, four arms and four legs wrapping me up in so much love I couldn't believe it.

Deft little fingers danced down my stomach and dipped between my thighs. "You're soaked," Chick said, awed as always that I get off on this.

Before I could retort, Master kissed me, then grabbed Chick by the hair. "Make her come—and make it good—then we can finish what we started."

With a wicked grin, she scrambled between my legs, all puppy-like excitement. We balance each other well.

Chick explored my folds with a finger, tracing along my pussy lips and around my clit, then sank her fingers deep into my cunt. I bucked off the bed, primed and ready. She fucked me with one, then two digits. That third, she held back until I begged—which I did, shamelessly.

Full, and edging toward that bone-rattling orgasm I knew awaited, I twined my fingers in her hair and pulled her lips against my clit. She lapped at it, the tease. "More, damn it. Chick, I need—"

She bit down on that sensitive nub, exactly what I craved. Pleasure, relief, jolted through my body. I arched off the bed, which Master saw as an invitation. He sank his teeth into the upper curve of my breast, marking me as I came.

I don't know how long I lay there, but when the room stopped spinning Chick was straddling me, her face tucked into the curve of my neck. I inhaled her sweet peach scent, a soft contrast to his spicy aftershave.

She clung to me as Master kept his promise and fucked her deep and slow. Her whimpers for *more* vibrated through my chest until he complied. Over her shoulder, he caught my eye and smiled.

A shudder ran through him. Chick bit down on my neck as he threw them off the edge of orgasm together, with me clinging to the edges of their bliss.

For the first time in weeks, surrounded by my loves, I slept uninterrupted through the night.

NEEDLES

Kathleen Tudor

My skin buzzed with energy as my Master escorted me into the smallish room we were supposed to use for our demo. Only about ten by twenty feet, the room was crowded with students who were eager to learn what my Master could teach them. He led me behind a small medical exam table that had been centered along the long wall, and nodded to me. With a smile, I turned my back on the group of milling students, and the noise in the room dropped appreciably as I lowered my bathrobe to the floor.

It wasn't strictly necessary for our needle demo, but I had a nearly perfect body—one I worked hours a day to maintain—and I was always looking for excuses to show it off to those inferior creatures who could dream of me but never have me. Only Master was worthy, of course.

I scooted onto the exam table, and the room quieted even more. I imagined the eyes roaming over my rounded ass and the smooth, soft curve of my spine. I straightened, wanting my posture to be perfect, and Master smirked at me. He appreciated the fruits of my vanity, but that didn't mean he didn't recognize it as vanity. I winked back at him, and with a small shake of his head, he placed the sharps container on the table beside me and began his lecture with an explanation of the proper health and safety procedures for working with needles.

He snapped gloves onto his hands as he talked, and I shuddered in anticipation, my eyes already going fuzzy as the routine sent me into the first hazy moments of subspace. Behind me, someone asked a question. I didn't even hear the words, as I was far too focused on the intoxicating smell of the rubbing alcohol as he uncapped the bottle. He said something about cleaning the skin, but I wasn't listening—he wasn't talking to me.

The cotton ball dragged a cold line across my chest just below the collarbone, and I dropped my head back with a small sigh of pleasure as he swabbed my skin clean. I heard a collective intake of breath from behind me and gave a dazed smile, still coherent enough to have my vanity stroked. *Yes...look all you want, but you can't touch.*

Master gave a quiet snort, and surreptitiously pinched one of my nipples, hard. I opened one eye and gave him a lazy, pleased smile. I was like a cat stretched out in my favorite sunny patch, knowing the day was only going to get better as I soaked it up. He was still talking about safety and disease transmission or something as he inserted the first needle, piercing the skin just below my left collarbone with a slender hypodermic tip, and sliding it under my flesh. I repressed a shudder of pleasure, exhaling completely as I waited for the needle to poke back up from under my skin and stop.

He released the needle, and I let the shudder loose. I could feel the syringe tip putting slight pressure on my skin where it punctured my flesh, tugging a little as I shifted. My pussy went from warm and pleasant to liquid gold. It wouldn't be long before I began to leave a little puddle on the exam table. The thought made me smile.

Master was still droning on about using fresh, sterile needles for each application, and suggesting places online where they could be purchased in packs of a hundred. I had never concerned myself with the details of where he got them; I just knew that I was safe and taken care of in his hands, and that it felt exquisite when my flesh was punctured and penetrated as he was doing now, the needle moving beneath the skin. A tiny, cold-steel fuck.

My mind was wavering on his words, which weren't meant for me, anyway; I gave a mental shrug and let them go. They washed over me, flooding me with meaningless sounds—a reassurance of his presence and attention, which required no focus or effort on my part. It was up to me to sit still and relax under his ministrations, nothing more.

His warm, gloved fingers pinched yet another fold of skin, this time on the opposite side of my chest, and I let out a moan as he slowly penetrated me, sinking deep into my body (or so it felt) before pushing the needle point back up through the skin and letting it go. My body tingled with heat and my pussy throbbed for attention. I could feel my clit swelling and straining, my thighs damp from the juices that flooded from me.

Another needle beneath the last, and my moan turned into a whimper of pleasure and a demand for more. My body trembled ever so slightly with desire and arousal and probably some chemical cocktail being released in my brain. The skin of my chest had begun to burn and ache in a dull, persistent way that provided powerful counterpoint to the sharp, piercing stabs assaulting my senses. Left, right, left, right—the line of needles marched down my chest from just beneath my collarbones, down my breasts.

Master was *still* lecturing about technique and safety precautions, or so I gathered from the occasional buzz of words that saw fit to translate themselves through my half-addled brain, but I was hardly paying any attention by now. I let the words flow around me, resenting the meaning that they tried to impose, wanting instead to simply flow on the rivers of pain and pleasure.

When Master pinched one peaked nipple and lifted it, I knew he was going to put a needle right through it; I moaned and squirmed at the mere thought. It would hurt more than any of the other needles, but it would be an incredible pleasure, too. My cunt clenched and gushed with arousal, and my breath was shallow and desperate.

He put the needle through, his hands firm and steady, and I let out a small scream of sheer torturous ecstasy. It was the closest I had ever come to orgasm without clitoral stimulation, and I was dying and desperate for the second side. *Do it! Pierce me! Penetrate me! Stick me until I scream!*

He pinched the second nipple, and I moaned and clenched my legs together. My thighs pressed together so hard that I felt the pressure on my clit, and took a deep breath, my mind just sharp enough to think—to plan.

When I felt the tip of the needle against my nipple, but before he pushed it through, I squeezed my legs as hard as I could. The steel slid through my nipple, and my entire body was struck with the pain/pleasure, which gathered and multiplied inside me, shot down to my clit in a bolt like lightning and was caught there and released by the pressure of my thighs. I screamed as the orgasm ripped through me, devastating and powerful and hard earned. My entire body seemed to ripple with the force of it, and I cried out as wave after wave of pleasure coursed through me like electrical current, stimulated to even greater heights with each needle it passed through.

It took what felt like a long time to come down from that pleasure and regain enough awareness of the room to recognize my Master's wry smile and the heavy breathing that filled the otherwise silent room, which was now pregnant with arousal and anticipation after my little display.

"As you can see," Master said, "needles can provide an incredibly intense and pleasurable stimulus to a sub who is inclined toward them." He pinched me playfully on the stomach, and I smiled dreamily at him, still half lost in subspace. My mind reeled toward him; my pussy suddenly ached to be filled.

"Master," I murmured dreamily. He put a hand firmly on my shoulder to keep me in place, but I wriggled beneath it, my hips rocking as I tried to invite him in.

Master chuckled. "Calm down, my dear. Extend your arm so that I can demonstrate technique."

I heard people gather behind us, shuffling closer in eager anticipation, but their anticipation was nothing compared to mine. I pushed toward him again, moaning in denial as I reached for him instead of extending my arm the way I knew he wanted me to. He sighed and pushed me back again. "Pay attention, my pet. Come back, now. It's time to show them—"

I shut him up with a kiss, not wanting this strange barrier of words, wanting only sensation, pleasant and painful and everything in between. He flicked one of the needles still piercing my nipples, and I yipped and jerked back, the pain clearing my head just a little. Not enough. I whimpered and yearned toward him again, and he sighed. With one firm hand on my chest, between the needles, Master pushed me backward until I was bent back over the exam table, my head and shoulders hanging upside down on the opposite side.

I smiled lazily at the people who stared hungrily at me on the other side of the table. My breasts had shifted, putting exquisite pressure on some of the penetration points and forcing the needles into new positions inside my flesh. I whimpered and shifted again as I prayed for fulfillment.

"I hope you'll all excuse me for a moment, but it seems my sub has gotten herself all worked up," Master said. *Oh, thank god!*

I heard his gloves snap off, then the jingle of his belt buckle and the tear of a condom wrapper. My eyes focused hazily on the crowd of upside-down people, who all stared at me as if I were some delicacy that they hoped to taste. *But you can't*, I thought, *only Master*. I moaned and spread my legs for him, and heard his voice faintly over the buzzing in my ears.

"With sex, as with needle play, caution and protection are always recommended." I imagined him sliding the condom on over his girth, and moaned. "And as with needle play, the method and speed of penetration contribute significantly to the experience." A few people in the crowd chuckled, but most of them were still staring, mesmerized, at my slender body or the twin tracks of needle tips that marched in a line from my collarbones down the front of each breast, now compacted with gravity's reversal.

Master penetrated me as steadily and easily as a needle through my flesh, sliding inside me in one smooth stroke that made me moan, long and low and hard. I contracted around him, squeezing encouragement as he filled me, and he rewarded me with a thumb on my clit, rubbing me toward another orgasm as he started to fuck me steadily. "And, of course, clitoral play can increase the pleasure for your sub, whatever other activities you are engaged in. Alternating needle insertion and clit stimulation can actually be an excellent way to calm a nervous or hesitant sub."

I was neither nervous, nor hesitant. I locked eyes with one particular woman wearing a black leather collar that hid most of the slim column of her neck. Her eyes were wide and dilated with arousal, and she licked her lips as my eyes fixed on hers. I grinned and watched her face, seeing my own pleasure reflected back in her eyes, and let the pleasure take me away as Master built cleverly on the sensations that already flooded me.

Each thrust of his cock sent a new wash of sensation through my body as the needles shifted and bumped. I closed my eyes and let myself fully experience every sensory variant. When I opened them again, several men were stroking large bulges in their trousers, and many of the women were wide-eyed and panting with desire, either for me or for their own release. It didn't matter—I let their desire fuel my own pleasure like it was being magnified.

I didn't hear the packet that Master must have torn open with his teeth. One moment I was riding on the edge of pleasure, and the next, Master removed his attentions from my clit and a second later I felt a sharp piercing pain in my labia as Master lifted them and pinned them together above my clit. It was too much. It was just enough. It was overwhelming and explosive and horrible and perfect, and I screamed bloody murder as the pain and pleasure drove me half out of my mind. My vision went dark for a moment. I screamed and screamed until I ran out of air, and then I panted and writhed as I tried to gather myself back together.

Distantly, I was aware of my Master fucking me harder. His cock thrusting into me made that last piercing burn and ache as he slammed against it and stretched it wide with his thrusts. He groaned in pleasure a moment later. I sagged with relief as he withdrew from me. I was satisfied, and I was exhausted.

As his careful hands cradled me a moment later, I felt myself being edged sideways until I lay completely upon the exam table, limp and spent.

A moment later I heard the snap of his gloves, then he lifted my arm. I heard him, still businesslike and professional, say, "Now, if you'll all gather closely, I'll demonstrate the proper technique for inserting and removing a needle, and then we can all do a little hands-on practice."

A bright prick of mild pain cut through my hazy, perfect world, and I absorbed it, smiling absently in the direction of the crowd as my Master penetrated me again with another tiny, cold-steel prick.

ADMITTING IT IS
THE FIRST STEP

Rachel Kramer Bussel

R yder can make anything kinky—even a twelve-step meeting.
Well, at least, one of the twelve steps. He's been going to AA
since long before I met him at a meeting three years ago. It's a
good thing, because I would've easily fallen for him no matter
how soon after I'd gotten sober. There's just something about
him that is so utterly compelling. He gives motivational speeches
as part of his work as a life coach, and is very out about being in
the program. I wasn't out when we met, but now I am, though
I keep a lower profile. What he isn't as public about is just how
filthy and perverted he is. That's our little secret. Or rather, big
secret, because like I said, he can and does fill our lives with
kink. He might make me change out of my bra and panties into
ones he's selected—or sometimes none at all—or summon me
to his office for a midday blow job (I'm a freelance copyeditor
who works from home). I never know what to expect, which is
part of the thrill.

Sometimes I think Ryder orders me to try things just because he knows he can get me to do them—that's his kink. I've learned never to say that I find someone unattractive because, just for kicks, that's who Ryder will tell that I am especially interested in him and would be honored to service him in whatever way Ryder sees fit, which is how I've wound up tied up in a coat closet and sniffing a runner's feet. They're not things I'd have chosen, but under Ryder's watchful eye I can still get off on them. I'm the first to admit that he always rewards me well for my obedience. He's the type of guy who'll tinker in the garage and rig a special sex toy to do exactly what I want it to, or snoop in my online wish lists and surprise me with a designer dress. He balances the sadistic with the sweet and can still make me instantly wet. There's no average night in our household or our bed. He knows I'm up for almost anything, and I trust him to never push me into something that's a hard limit.

But the edges of those limits are where his dirty mind tends to gravitate. It seems to ratchet up on holidays—he's bought me nipple clamps with bells for Christmas, spanked hearts into my ass with a paddle for Valentine's Day and kept a ball gag in my mouth for almost an entire birthday. So for my recent sober anniversary, he gives me a little drill, a perversion of the twelve-step process in every sense of the word. "Now, what I'm about to say is not to be shared. I love the fact that you're as perverted as I am and don't think of it as a problem, but I was thinking about all the progress you've made on yourself since you stopped drinking. I didn't know you before, but I'd bet money that sobriety makes you a better girlfriend, and a better sub. So I'm twisting the rules a little, and now you're doing my steps, for me—think of me as your higher power when it comes to kink, which I hope you already do. What I want is, for the next week you tell anyone you encounter when you're with me that you're my sub. I want you to own it, be proud of it, say it out loud. Admit it—because it's such a big part of who you are."

I'm floored, not least of all because if I were to admit that very thing with him next to me, I'll be outing him as well. It's so absurd it's almost laughable—until I see the searing look he's giving me and realize there's nothing to joke about. My man is as serious as a heart attack, the intensity so real it's almost visible. We are so much a part of each other's minds, he can tell exactly what I'm thinking, and he acknowledges it right back. "It's okay, I'm a big boy—I can take it. Yes, it means coming out, but I won't make you do it everywhere. Not to colleagues, not in front of anyone who might make your life more difficult. That's not what this is about. But you're going to get used to saying it, if you want what comes with me owning you."

I lick my lips, fire rushing through me at the very thought. I love being a brat, and am sure plenty of vanilla people we know have guessed the true nature of our relationship. But there's flirty guessing, and then there's outright admissions. "So what exactly do you want me to say?"

"I'll be there to coach you, don't worry. You just have to say exactly what I tell you to. If you get totally stuck the first few times, I'll jump in and rescue you—but be warned, you may find that a worse alternative. Now come on, get ready, we're going out."

It isn't dinnertime, but that's never stopped Ryder from eating. I check that I look okay; my tousled strawberry-blonde hair hangs just past my shoulders, streaks from the summer sun making it even lighter than usual. My only makeup is shiny pink lip gloss—Ryder prefers me fresh faced, even though when he met me I was in full glam mode. I've found it far more rewarding to give the man what he wants, because he will then give me everything I want, even the things I don't yet know I want until he provides them. My fingers instinctively move to the initials at the base of my neck: R.S. RYDER'S SLUT. He'd sworn up and down he'd never asked another woman to get that tattooed when he proposed it to me after a scene that made both our hearts pound so loudly the noise was all I could hear.

It had taken a year for me to even consider it—how ridiculous would I, Caitlin Conners, look if we broke up? How could I explain R.S.? But that was just one of the many things I'd done, initially for him, and only later appreciated its value to me.

What he wants now is akin to tattooing those words in full across my face. I've never been shy about how much of a masochist I am, but I've also never walked up to perfect strangers and given them a glimpse into my kink. "Smile, sweetheart. Don't tell me you're not turned on," he says, inching forward until he's directly in front of me. The throbbing between my legs increases as he narrows the space between us. I'm sure he'll want to touch me to find out, but just when I expect him to do something, Ryder does the opposite.

"Maybe," I reply, though the truth is surely written all over my face.

"Well, ready or not, here we come. Oh wait—you need to put this on." The hot-pink blindfold has *Slut* written across the front in elegant black cursive.

I open my mouth to say, "You really expect me to wear that?" but just as quickly shut it. Ryder never says anything he doesn't mean—each word is carefully thought out, its meaning pondered, until what leaves his lips is a carefully massaged message. My protesting would just get me a slap across the face—something, let me be clear, I love, that would only make me even wetter. Still, it would mean I'd disobeyed him, so I wouldn't truly be able to enjoy it. As it is, the seam of my tight jeans is already a little uncomfortable as it presses against my center. So I turn around and let him slip the blindfold over my head.

Our apartment building has a garage, and I can count on one hand how many times I've run into anyone in there during the day, but still, I'm sure today will be the day every single one of our neighbors is congregating there, shooting the shit, while their slutty fellow apartment dweller is led out the door by her own personal Christian Grey. Sure, they've probably heard me crying out or getting spanked—though Ryder is good about gagging me when he thinks I'll make too much noise— but again, what they can guess at might provide a frisson of sexual excitement. What they know for sure is just gossip to be passed around—the way, for all I know, Ryder is about to pass me around.

I follow him, my hand clutching his tightly, trying to be as quiet as possible—so of course I crash into something that falls noisily to the ground. "Just stay there, C, I'll get it." He does so but manages to make even more noise—it sounds even louder with one of my senses out of play.

Eventually we make it to the car; he helps me in, thoroughly checking that I'm buckled in, with detours under my top directly to my nipples and one all too brief brush between my legs. "You get to pick the music, since you can't see," he says.

"Pearl Jam," I request, my hand automatically reaching for the CD case on the floor, even though I won't be able to see what's inside it. I've shut my eyes on car trips with him, but I've never had them shut from the get-go, never been unable to flutter my lashes and take in what's before me. It's unnerving, but exciting too.

The AC is on, but a few minutes in, while we're stopped, I hear my window rolling down and Ryder says, "Turn to your right and give the nice man a big smile. Show him what a slut you are." Oh my goodness. We're starting already, not five minutes from our home. What if I know this person? Maybe on my own wearing the mask, my identity would've been hidden, but I'm with Ryder, and anyone who knows me knows I'm with him. That I'm his, even if they don't know how fully his I truly am.

Even though my face burns, I know, and am sure Ryder knows, that I get insanely wet as I turn and smile at whoever is next to us. *Maybe it's nobody, maybe he's just faking me out,* I think, before I hear two quick beeps and a whistle. I have to admit, if only to myself, though, that underneath the humiliation is a bit of fun. Only Ryder could think of something so depraved.

Finally, after what feels like an hour but, when my eyes are freed, I see has only been twenty minutes, we pull over to a roadside stand—a hot-dog stand, of course. "I'll tell you what to say," Ryder tells me, before kissing me deeply.

I walk in front of him, his hand on my lower back guiding me. I'm no longer wearing the blindfold, but my sluthood feels emblazoned on my face. The place is doing a brisk business; Ryder either lucked out or has picked this time for maximum effect. After a couple orders hot dogs with the works, I'm next. "What'll it be, sweetheart?" a man who looks to be in his mid-fifties asks with a wink.

I don't even look at the menu, because Ryder has already whispered in my ear what I'm to say. "Two of the extra-large sausages—I like them nice and juicy." I want to laugh, but I also know that Ryder could put his hand between my legs right now and find out just how seriously I'm taking this. "I can fit a lot in my mouth." I try to muster a flirtatious tone, and am rewarded with a huge grin from the man, his fingers lingering extra long on mine when I hand over the five dollars. I can't believe I've just said that, but Ryder's light pinch of my hip lets me know I've done a good job.

I smile uncertainly and then go to wait at a table with Ryder.

"Sausage is your favorite food, isn't it, honey?" he asks in a louder tone than normal. "You certainly like mine."

I hear a chuckle nearby. My cheeks are flaming—I can always tell—but I sit there and let Ryder joke around about my big mouth. When our giant sausages are placed on the table, he makes a show of pushing both to my side. "They're for her— she's extra hungry today." Then he leans across and says, "Make sure they know how much you can take."

I can be defiant when I want to be, and just to show Ryder, I proceed to make eye contact with an older man sitting at a nearby table and then lick the head of the sausage, before slowly placing the tip in my mouth. I'd eased the bun down so all I am now putting between my lips is the sausage itself, which is delightfully spicy. I close my eyes and make an orgasmic sound as I bite into it in a way that makes juice drip down my chin. "Oops," I giggle, sticking out my tongue to lick it off, before using a napkin. I proceed to thoroughly enjoy each of the sausages, even though they're so big, one would've been fine.

I hear Ryder whisper, "You are making quite a scene, my dear. I hope you really are hungry for my sausage when we get home." I could swear I hear someone say, "Damn," under his breath at that.

When I'm done, he walks over and grabs me roughly by the hair, then kisses me hard. I'm shaking a little when I stand up. I can't mistake the whistles and claps I get as I head back into the car.

This time I don't question the blindfold; in fact, I'm happy to put it on again, now that I've proven just how slutty I am. "That was easy. Those were strangers. Now you're going to have to tell someone you will be seeing again."

I shiver despite the heat, barely hearing the music I let Ryder select this time. He gives me space to think, to contemplate my outing as a slut, a whore—as his. In truth, being fully his, belonging to him, is my proudest accomplishment, but despite that, I've clung to our privacy out of my own fetish for secrecy. It seemed to coincide with his. Now that he's changed, my job, if I'm truly to belong to him, is to change with him.

So when we pull up in front of our dry cleaners and he removes the blindfold, I don't flinch, even though I'm there at least once a week. Ryder hands me a ticket and smirks. I wouldn't have thought he even knew where the dry cleaners was located; I'm the one who takes his suits in to be pressed. "You know what to tell Mr. Foster, right?"

I nod, tempted to back out all of a sudden. Instead I march right in. "Hi Mr. Foster," I greet the kindly owner. "I'm here to pick this up for Ryder...and he wants me to tell you I'm his kinky slave. I do whatever he tells me to. Usually in the bedroom but today, outside of it too." I say it as fast as I can, hoping maybe he won't pick up on the nuances, even though my face is burning again.

"That would explain it," he says slowly, staring right back at me. I hand him the ticket, a spark generating for the first time ever with him when our hands touch.

He goes to the back and returns with the skimpiest of lingerie, all wrapped in plastic. When I look closer I see it's a pale-purple teddy with cutouts for the nipples and the crotch wide open. I almost laugh—it's got to be new and there's no way it needed dry-cleaning—but I catch myself when Mr. Foster says, "I hope you make good use of it."

I pay in cash, leaving a generous tip, because even I can't stop to wait for the change. "Like your present?" is all Ryder says when I get back in the car.

"Oh my god, that was so embarrassing."

"But it turned you on, didn't it? To know that he knows you're going to wear this for me?"

"Yes, Ryder," I admit, because I can never deny him the truth about what gets me wet.

"One more stop. I'll come in with you."

With a few turns, we pull in front of the lingerie shop we've spent hundreds of dollars in. "Take it with you. I'll even do the talking."

Ryder is true to his words—it's his turn to admit what we really are to each other. Stella, the saleswoman who's had her hands all over my body in the name of intimate apparel, beams at us. "She likes it, and wants to try it on to make sure it fits. Don't you, honey?"

"Yes," I say, catching Stella's appraising eye. Is that a hint of admiration—or perhaps envy—I see there?

Ryder leads me to the back dressing room, which isn't really built for two, but no matter. I strip naked, then slip on the skimpy purple outfit. My nipples look obscenely large poking out from the fabric and my sex is on full display. "Stella, can you bring us some nylons and a pair of heels?" Ryder calls out.

In what feels like seconds, Stella is kneeling below me, her head inches from my pussy, fastening the garters to the white fishnets and then slipping my feet into five-inch Lucite stripper heels. I look ridiculous, but I feel on fire. "Good job, Stella," Ryder says in the deep voice I thought he reserved just for me. But instead of being jealous, I'm wet as can be.

"You should know, Stella, that Caitlin is my slave. She does whatever I tell her to. She's all mine. But she's been very good today, better than I could have anticipated, and I think she deserves a treat. Would you like to use our new riding crop on her?" He walks forward and presses Stella against the pretty rose wallpaper.

"I would," she says, her voice trembling. "I just need to put the DO NOT DISTURB sign up."

"You better hurry or I'll have to work her over myself. I just can't wait until we get home." He tugs on each nipple, and I have to reach for the wall so I don't collapse.

Stella returns with a three-hundred-dollar, rhinestone-studded riding crop and a wicked smile on her face. "You're almost ready. Just give me your panties, Stella." She blushes furiously, but she hands them over. Ryder promptly stuffs them in my mouth and hands me the car keys. "Drop these if you want it to stop," he says.

He then stands behind Stella, remarkably nimble in the small space, and shows her how and where to stroke me with the crop. Of course he makes me face them, rather than allowing me the dignity of closing my eyes. She's either a fast learner or a sadist herself, because her blows against my hard nipples hurt in the most glorious way. I'm shaking, tears forming, as the accumulation of the day's intensity hits me right along with the tip of the crop. Through the mirror on the door, I see his hand cupping her ass as she strikes my inner thighs. "Spread your legs wider," Ryder tells me. I suddenly wish for something hanging from the ceiling to hold on to. Stella hits my thighs and my pussy until I'm barely holding it together. Finally, Ryder stills her hand. "Thank you for your help, Stella, from me and my slave."

"You're very welcome," she says, the look on her face one of pure admiration.

"What do you say, Caitlin?" he asks, yanking the panties out of my mouth and shoving them in his pocket.

"Thank you, Stella. I'm glad you know that I'm Ryder's to control," I add impromptu.

"Now if you'll excuse us, this little slut deserves a good fucking."

Ryder allows me to slip on a nightie that barely covers me, and pays for all of it, including the shoes. I totter out the door in the getup, sure that anyone who doesn't yet know who I am deep down will be able to tell if they look at me in this moment, marching to the car in these slutty shoes and lingerie. I don't look down or cower; I walk tall and proud. I'd go anywhere and do anything for Ryder, and I don't care who knows it.

ABOUT THE AUTHORS

VALERIE ALEXANDER lives in Arizona. Her work has been previously published in *Best of Best Women's Erotica, Best Bondage Erotica* and other anthologies.

EMILY BINGHAM is a Portland, Oregon, author, whose writing has appeared in *Best Bondage Erotica 2011, Serving Him: Tales of Erotic Submission*, and on Cleansheets.com. She's also a fetish model for photographers across the country. Her adventures in rope can be found at her erotic writing blog queanofrope.com.

ERZABET BISHOP (Twitter @erzabetbishop) has been crafting stories since she could first pound keys on her parents' old typewriter, but only discovered recently that writing naughty books is much more fun. She is a contributing author to *Coming Together: Girl on Girl* along with many other anthologies.

JACQUELINE BROCKER (jacquelinebrocker.esquinx.net) is an Australian writer living in the United Kingdom. Her short erotic fiction has appeared in *My First Spanking, The Mammoth Book of Quick and Dirty Erotica* and *Under Her Thumb* (Cleis Press). Her novella *Body & Bow* was published by Forbidden Fiction.

KATHLEEN DELANEY-ADAMS is a stone high femme porn author and spoken word performer. A national touring veteran, Kathleen is the artistic director of BODY HEAT: Femme Porn Tour, now in its seventh year. Look for her work in *Best Bondage Erotica 2014*, edited by Rachel Kramer Bussel.

JUSTINE ELYOT isn't sure how she managed to write twelve erotic novels since 2008 but somehow it happened, and it's still happening now. She's also written dozens of novellas and short stories for publishers such as Black Lace, Cleis, Mischief and Xcite, among others. BDSM is number one in her top ten of favorite themes.

DOROTHY FREED (dorothyfreedwrites.com; @Dorothy-Freed1) is the pseudonym of an artist turned writer who lives near San Francisco, and writes both fiction and memoir. Her work appears in *Cheeky Spanking Stories, Twice the Pleasure, Ageless Erotica, The Seattle Art and Literature Festival 10th Anniversary Anthology* and *The Mammoth Book of Quick and Dirty Erotica*.

LEIGH EDWARD GRAY is a brat who is learning to be good in Texas with her spouse. She enjoys cooking (and sometimes serving), reading and writing, and everything depicted in her work.

NIK HAVERT is a writer, horror-movie host and martial arts instructor. Some of his work has appeared in *Best Lesbian Erotica 2010, Girl Fever,* and *Twice the Pleasure* writing as Nicole Wolfe. He also writes and self-publishes comic books for models and adult film stars.

ELISE HEPNER writes smutty goodness for Ellora's Cave, Xcite and Secret Cravings Publishing. She's appeared in several Cleis anthologies including *Gotta Have It: 69 Stories of Sudden Sex* and *Best Bondage Erotica 2012.* She lives with her husband and two clingy kitties in Maryland.

TILLY HUNTER is a British author with a wicked imagination and a taste for quirky erotica. She has stories in anthologies from Xcite Books, MLR Press, House of Erotica and others. Her first solo e-book, *Miranda's Tempest: Three Classic Tales with a Kinky Twist,* is out now.

SKYLAR KADE (skylarkade.com) writes erotic romance of the kinky persuasion. She lives in California and spends her time asking the cabana boys to bring her more mimosas and feed her strawberries while she dreams up her next naughty adventure.

D. L. KING (dlkingerotica.blogspot.com) is the editor of anthologies such as *Slave Girls, Under Her Thumb* and *The Harder She Comes,* winner of the Lambda Literary Award and the Independent Publisher's Book Award gold medal. Her stories can be found in *Best Bondage Erotica, Leather Ever After* and *Luscious,* among others.

MINA MURRAY (minamurray.wordpress.com) is an antipodean whiskey aficionado and smut-peddler. Her work is featured in several anthologies, including *Brief Encounters*; *Sudden Sex: 69 Sultry Short Stories*; *The Mammoth Book of Quick & Dirty Erotica*; *Baby Got Back* and *The Big Book of Orgasms*.

GISELLE RENARDE is a queer Canadian, avid volunteer, contributor to more than one hundred short-story anthologies, and award-winning author of books like *Anonymous, The Red Satin Collection* and *My Mistress' Thighs*. Ms. Renarde lives across from a park with two bilingual cats who sleep on her head.

ALVA ROSE has been writing since she could speak. Her smut is informed by a strong set of sex-positive feminist values and attempts to model the best of our sexual culture while still getting you off. She resides in the snowy city of Rochester, NY, and tweets at @alvarosewrites.

MORGAN SIERRA (deecarney.com) is the pen name for award-winning, best-selling author, Dee Carney. Morgan's erotica pushes boundaries and are stories that are a little hotter, a little naughtier and a lot more sensual.

KATHLEEN TUDOR is a rockin' erotic author and super-editor, with stories in anthologies from Cleis, Circlet, Storm Moon, Mischief HarperCollins, Xcite and more. Check out *Take Me* and *My Boyfriend's Boyfriends*. Want to feature in your own erotic short? Email PolyKathleen@gmail.com for details.

JADE A. WATERS (jadeawaters.com) began her literary naughtiness when she convinced her boyfriend that the sexiest form of foreplay was reading provocative synonyms from a thesaurus.

Her latest piece, "The Flogger," can be found in *The Big Book of Orgasms* from Cleis Press.

SARA TAYLOR WOODS (sarataylorwoods.com; @sarataylorwoods) writes erotica and dark contemporary fantasy. Her short story, "A Girl's Gotta Eat," appeared in *The Big Bad*, and her erotic short, "Well Suited," was featured on bestselling author Tiffany Reisz's blog.

ABOUT
THE EDITOR

RACHEL KRAMER BUSSEL (rachelkramerbussel.com) is a New Jersey–based author, editor and blogger. She has edited over fifty books of erotica, including *Anything for You: Erotica for Kinky Couples; Best Bondage Erotica 2011, 2012, 2013, 2014* and *2015; The Big Book of Orgasms; Baby Got Back: Anal Erotica; Come Again: Sex Toy Erotica; Suite Encounters; Going Down; Irresistible; Gotta Have It; Obsessed; Women in Lust; Surrender; Orgasmic; Cheeky Spanking Stories; Bottoms Up; Spanked: Red-Cheeked Erotica; Fast Girls; Flying High; Do Not Disturb; Going Down; Tasting Him; Tasting Her; Please, Sir; Please, Ma'am; He's on Top; She's on Top; Caught Looking; Hide and Seek; Crossdressing* and *Lust in Latex.* Her anthologies have won eight IPPY (Independent Publisher) Awards, and *Surrender* won the National Leather Association Samois Anthology Award. Her work has been published in over one hundred anthologies, including *Best American Erotica 2004* and *2006.* She wrote the popular "Lusty Lady" column for the *Village Voice* and currently writes columns for

Philadelphia City Paper and *DAME*. Rachel has written for *AVN, Bust,* Cleansheets.com, *Cosmopolitan, Curve,* The Daily Beast, TheFrisky.com, *Glamour,* Gothamist, *Harper's Bazaar,* Huffington Post, *Inked, Marie Claire,* Mediabistro, *Newsday, New York Post, New York Observer, The New York Times, O, The Oprah Magazine, Penthouse,* The Root, Salon, *San Francisco Chronicle, Time Out New York, The Washington Post* and *Zink,* among others. She has appeared on "The Gayle King Show," "The Martha Stewart Show," "The Berman and Berman Show," NY1 and Showtime's "Family Business." She hosted the popular In the Flesh Erotic Reading Series, featuring readers from Susie Bright to Zane, and speaks at conferences, does readings and teaches erotic writing workshops across the country. She blogs at lustylady.blogspot.com and tweets @raquelita.